BM-2022

"What do you want from me, John?" Lauren asked.

"To trust me. To believe that I have staying power," he replied.

"I don't understand what you mean."

He shook his head. "It doesn't matter. I think you're a lady who has to be shown. Time will take care of that."

She stood up. "We have one more day at the cottage. That's all the time you have."

She had taken only a few steps when he came after her. He whirled her around and pulled her against him. Lowering his head, he murmured, "Then I better not waste another minute."

His mouth covered hers, and his hungry demand rocked her senses. A shiver of response ran through her as the kiss deepened, and she was drawn into the primitive realm of passion. . . .

Northern Illinois Largest & Lowest
Priced Paperback Selection
We Buy, Sell & Trade
Books, Comics, Records
Galaxy of Books
1908
Zion,
312 -
D1410159

WHAT ARE *LOVESWEPT* ROMANCES?

They are stories of true romance and touching emotion. We believe those two very important ingredients are constants in our highly sensual and very believable stories in the *LOVESWEPT* line. Our goal is to give you, the reader, stories of consistently high quality that may sometimes make you laugh, sometimes make you cry, but are always fresh and creative and contain many delightful surprises within their pages.

Most romance fans read an enormous number of books. Those they truly love, they keep. Others may be traded with friends and soon forgotten. We hope that each *LOVESWEPT* romance will be a treasure—a "keeper." We will always try to publish

LOVE STORIES YOU'LL NEVER FORGET
BY AUTHORS YOU'LL ALWAYS REMEMBER

The Editors

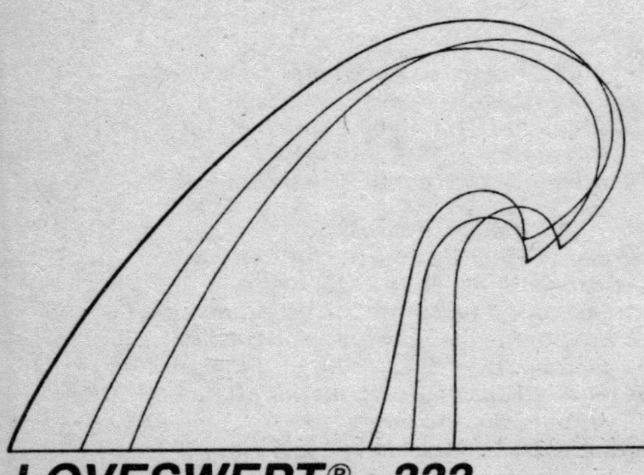

LOVESWEPT® • 333

Patt Bucheister

Fire and Ice

BANTAM BOOKS
NEW YORK • TORONTO • LONDON • SYDNEY • AUCKLAND

FIRE AND ICE

A Bantam Book / June 1989

LOVESWEPT® and the wave device are registered trademarks of Bantam Books, a division of Bantam Doubleday Dell Publishing Group, Inc. Registered in U.S. Patent and Trademark Office and elsewhere.

All rights reserved.
Copyright © 1989 by Patt Bucheister.
Cover art copyright © 1989 by Enric.
No part of this book may be reproduced or transmitted in any form or by any means, electronic or mechanical, including photocopying, recording, or by any information storage and retrieval system, without permission in writing from the publisher.
For information address: Bantam Books.

If you would be interested in receiving protective vinyl covers for your Loveswept books, please write to this address for information:

Loveswept
Bantam Books
P.O. Box 985
Hicksville, NY 11802

ISBN 0-553-21995-2

Published simultaneously in the United States and Canada

Bantam Books are published by Bantam Books, a division of Bantam Doubleday Dell Publishing Group, Inc. Its trademark, consisting of the words "Bantam Books" and the portrayal of a rooster, is Registered in U.S. Patent and Trademark Office and in other countries. Marca Registrada. Bantam Books, 666 Fifth Avenue, New York, New York 10103.

PRINTED IN THE UNITED STATES OF AMERICA

O 0 9 8 7 6 5 4 3 2 1

One

A paper airplane soared gracefully through the air and collided with the solid chest of the man who had just entered the room.

It was the last thing John Zachary expected when he opened the door to his office. He bent down and picked up the object that had fallen at his feet. As he examined it he could see portions of his letterhead on the bashed fuselage. Looking around, he saw that the plane that had hit him was not the only one that had taken flight. There were paper planes on his desk, the carpet, the glass coffee table.

Even more curious than having his office stationery flown about the room was the sight of a woman's shapely rear end protruding from beneath one of the end tables. She was on her hands and knees, apparently reaching for a crashed plane. Unfortunately the limited view gave him no clue to her identity. He was intrigued enough by what he could observe to want to see the rest of her. Her tantalizing movements stretched her red skirt snugly over her shapely curves, stirring his imagination.

He hadn't the faintest idea who the woman was, but he didn't have any problem identifying the other person responsible for the transformation of his office. The small child sitting on the plush gray carpet near his desk was his three-year-old daughter, Amy.

He was about to ask Amy why she was in his office when an unusual sound stopped him. She laughed. She was looking up at him, her hand covering her mouth as though laughing at her father were something to hide. On a scale of one-to-ten, the giggle rated a two, but it was the first time in the last three days he had seen any sign of amusement from her. He wouldn't have minded a hundred paper planes hitting him if it made her laugh again.

The woman under the table was obviously unaware of his presence. "We're going to have to make a new starship *Enterprise*, Amy," she called. "This one has a crushed nose."

"Okay. I can make it."

Amy picked up the partially folded paper in her lap. Her tongue appeared between her lips as she concentrated on folding another airplane. John saw that her blond hair had been plaited into two untidy braids by Mrs. Hamish. When he had picked Amy up at the airport, her silky hair had been arranged in a french braid, a coiffure too elaborate for the older woman he had hired to take care of her during the day. At the time he had thought that hairstyle was too old for her anyway, but this one wasn't much better. Amy's clothing also seemed wrong for the child. All of the dresses in the two suitcases that had arrived with her were similar to the one she wore today, pink with rows of ruffles and yards of lace trim. Expensive and formal and fussy. Like his ex-wife.

John heard the animation in his daughter's voice and marveled at the change in her. Since his ex-wife had virtually dropped Amy in his lap three days ago, the child had rarely spoken. He expected it would take Amy time to adjust to the abrupt changes in her life, but it was difficult to see her so quiet and withdrawn. Though admittedly not an expert on children, he didn't think her behavior was normal. He hadn't the faintest idea what she was doing in his office, but he was pleased to hear her laugh and to see her playing instead of sitting and staring off into space.

He wondered what magic the woman with the charming posterior had used.

Closing the door behind him, he asked, "Can I help?"

There was an abrupt thud as the woman in red hit her head on the table. She made a sound of pain and a few seconds later scooted out from under the table, sat back on her heels, and rubbed the back of her head as she scowled up at him.

Lauren McLean dropped her hand. It would be him, she thought. It couldn't have been his secretary finding her crawling around on the floor. It had to be John Zachary. Of all the people in Norfolk, why did it have to be him? She answered her own question: Because it was his office.

He was about six inches taller than her own five feet eight inches. At the moment, however, he towered over her, a puzzled expression in his dark eyes. His hair, his eyes, his suit and tie were all the color of rich dark coffee. Most of the time—like right now—his features looked as if they were carved out of granite. He was a man who smiled rarely, although his eyes would register amusement occasionally. His appearance was only part of the package. He was self-confident without being arrogant, radiating power and authority as easily as breathing. In her experience working for him, Lauren had found him to be tough, yet fair. He believed in hiring people who were the best at what they did, then leaving them alone to do it.

She gave him a weak smile. "Hello, Mr. Zachary."

His eyes narrowed as he stared at her. "Mac?"

How flattering, she thought. He wasn't sure who she was. Feeling ridiculous in her position on the floor, she stood up. A little dignity and decorum would be appropriate under the circumstances, she decided, if a bit late. Crawling around on his floor wasn't the professional image she preferred to present her employer. After all, she was only a little fish in the corporate pond John Zachary owned.

"Actually," she said, "my name is Lauren. I always thought Mac sounded like a bulldog or a truck, but I've never had a choice. It's a nickname I've been stuck with off and on all my life."

John blinked in surprise. "You'll have to forgive me for not recognizing you right away. I don't remember ever seeing that side of you before."

At first Lauren didn't understand what he was referring to. Then his gaze shifted to the table she had just been under. Refusing to be embarrassed, she said coolly, "You're forgiven. Besides, my backside is not one of my better features."

A corner of his mouth curved upward. "I wouldn't say that. I was suitably impressed."

She smiled faintly, acknowledging his backhanded compliment. It seemed fate had given her a birthday present by handing her one of her fantasies, she mused. She had never seen John smile before, and especially not at her. It dawned on her she was staring at his mouth, and she looked away.

The skirt of her linen dress had been crumpled during her excursion under the table. She ran her palms over the material several times, wondering how to make a graceful exit.

John's gaze followed the movements of her hands, and he was startled by the stirring in his body. Such a simple everyday gesture on her part, yet his thoughts had turned to imagining how her hands would feel flowing over him instead of her skirt. He looked away.

Carefully stepping around several of the paper planes on the carpet, he walked over to his desk and sat his briefcase on it. He gazed down at his daughter. "Hello, Amy."

As usual, the child simply stared back at him without responding.

Forcing down the disappointment that was becoming too familiar, he perched on the edge of his desk, crossing his arms over his chest. His dark gaze returned to Lauren.

She was tall and slender, with shiny ash blonde hair and smooth tanned skin. But it was her expressive light brown eyes that intrigued him and held his attention. She had the most alive eyes he had ever seen. It was odd that he hadn't noticed them before. Or maybe it wasn't so surprising, since the only times he ever saw her were during contract conferences and occasionally in the coffee shop downstairs. She had always been professional and businesslike with him. With others, he had noticed, she would smile, joke, and laugh, but not with him. Never with him. She was polite but distant, and he had the impression she didn't care for him.

The knowledge had bruised his pride, especially

because he found her intriguing. There was something about her that pulled at him like an invisible force, a strange attraction that drew his gaze to her whenever he saw her. Unfortunately she apparently didn't feel the same.

He brought his attention back to the matter at hand. "I'm curious about why you've turned my office into an airport."

"Making paper airplanes was the only thing I could think of to keep your daughter entertained." She glanced around. "Your office is very attractive and efficient, but there isn't a great deal in it for a child to play with."

He thought he detected a note of criticism and was amused. "Strangely enough, it's never been a problem until now. Let me rephrase the question. Why are you here with Amy? She's supposed to be home with a babysitter."

Lauren tucked a strand of her shoulder-length hair behind her ear. "Is the babysitter a woman about my height, reddish brown hair cut short with dull scissors, and talks like a machine gun?"

Although slightly unorthodox, her description fit Mrs. Hamish perfectly. He nodded. "Where did you see Mrs. Hamish?"

"I was returning from lunch when a woman stopped me outside the entrance to the building. She asked if I knew you, and I told her I knew who you were. Then before I blinked, she brought Amy out from behind her and instructed me to see that she got to your office. I'm supposed to tell you there was a family emergency in Philadelphia. Or was it Pittsburgh?" She shrugged. "I guess it doesn't matter. Anyway, that's all she said before she climbed into a taxi waiting at the curb."

Damn, he cursed silently. With Mrs. Hamish gone, he had no one to take care of Amy.

Lauren went on with her explanation. "I brought Amy up here, but your secretary said you were out of the office. I didn't want Amy to stay alone, so I remained here with her. I hope you don't mind."

"Of course not. I appreciate it." He glanced down at Amy, who was still folding paper into the shape of an airplane. "She seems to be enjoying herself." He returned his attention to Lauren. "How did Mrs. Hamish happen to choose you to take Amy?"

A glint of mischief flickered in her tawny eyes. "I was the only one she had to pick from. Everyone else had returned from lunch."

John stared at her shining eyes, then his gaze dropped to her mouth. "You were late?"

"Well, I have an excuse. Sort of. I'm sure Mr. Simpson won't agree with me." Simpson was the head of the contract department. John had his own opinion of the man and didn't make any comment. She continued, "Some friends of mine treated me to lunch. It happens to be my birthday. They brought a cake to a restaurant at The Waterside,"—she named Norfolk's trendy harbor area—"and I couldn't very well leave before I'd blown out the candles."

She had a fascinating mouth, John thought, especially when she smiled. He dragged his gaze back up to her eyes. "Were there all that many candles to blow out?"

"Enough," she said dryly. "Anyway, that's why I was late. You're the last one I should admit that to, but look at it this way—If I hadn't been there, Amy could have been turned over to the security guard instead."

"That's true." After a moment he added as an afterthought, "Happy birthday."

"Thanks," she muttered. Her birthday was not something she wanted to talk about right now. This was her twenty-ninth birthday, which meant in one more year she would be thirty. It was a milestone she was in no hurry to pass.

She began gathering up the folded papers scattered around his office. "Amy, how about helping me pick up the paper planes before I leave? We've made a mess of your father's office. Let's throw away the ones that crashed. If you want, you can keep the ones that will still fly."

Amy obeyed. With her arms full of planes, she asked, "Can't we make any more?"

Lauren smiled down at the child. "You can make them with your daddy now. I need to get back to work."

She saw Amy glance warily at her father, clearly unenthusiastic at the prospect of making paper airplanes with her father. Lauren looked at John Zachary, noting the guarded expression in his eyes. He didn't look any happier than Amy, which made Lauren wonder about their relationship. Then she quickly reminded herself it was none of her business.

John had also seen the lack of pleasure in his daughter's face. "Amy," he said, "you keep playing with the airplanes for a while longer. I want to talk to Mac."

Lauren didn't like the sound of that. "I really should be getting back to work, Mr. Zachary. I don't imagine Mr. Simpson is too happy with me at the moment. You know how he is about punctuality."

"I'll take care of Simpson."

"That's not necessary." She knew her department head wouldn't appreciate the boss excusing her absence from work. Simpson took great pride in his position of authority and wouldn't like one of his clerks going over his head.

"It was because of my daughter you were late, Mac," John said reasonably. "The least I can do is make sure you don't have any trouble with your supervisor."

She shook her head. "No thanks." She couldn't tell her employer that he would be causing her problems instead of solving them. Mr. Simpson was not her biggest fan to begin with, since she had taken the job he had promised to the brother of his current girlfriend. At least that was the theory provided by several of her co-workers who had noticed the supervisor's overt animosity toward her.

Thinking of how late she was already, Lauren decided it was time to make an exit. Besides, so much proximity to John Zachary might have her staring at him like some love-starved groupie. She kissed Amy's cheek before walking to the door. "Good-bye, Amy." She swept out of the office, closing the door firmly behind her.

She smiled at John's secretary, who looked up from the letter she was typing. Mrs. Murray had been obviously relieved when Lauren had offered to stay with Amy. An efficient secretary, Mrs. Murray could cope with juggling innumerable appointments, miles of dictation, and keeping up with a demanding employer, but the sight of a small child had clearly flustered her.

Lauren walked past the secretary and left the plush outer office, making a conscious effort not to hurry. Her heels made no sound on the thick-carpeted corridor as she headed toward the elevator. When the doors opened, she was relieved to see no one else was inside. She sagged against the wall of the elevator after the doors closed, shutting her eyes as she took a deep steadying breath.

It was odd how fate worked, she mused. Within an hour of declaring an end to her foolish romantic notions about John Zachary, she had become involved with his daughter and indirectly with him. Earlier, as she had walked back from her birthday celebration at The Waterside, she had declared her twenty-ninth birthday as good a time as any to review the past and plan for the future. There wasn't a single thing she could do about the past, but the future was up to her. She had decided she might as well get on with it.

It was ridiculous to be infatuated with a man she saw only occasionally during business hours. Their sole relationship was a professional one, with a slim chance of it's ever becoming anything else. She had always been cool and distant toward him to keep him or anyone else from guessing how she really felt.

Maybe her brother was right. He told her she never took the easy way out, no matter what she did. He said she had always desired the unattainable, like the time she had wanted the apple at the top of the tree rather than settling for any that were easier to pick. That particular time she had ended up falling out of the tree and breaking her arm. This time she could break her heart.

Her feelings for John Zachary had grown steadily in the year she had worked for his company. Like every other woman in the building, she had been attracted by his quiet charm blended with the subtle power ingrained in his personality. As the days passed she found her emotions deepening beyond an admiration for an intelligent mind and a virile body. Her attraction had grown like a stubborn flower that could bud and blossom without receiving any nourishment.

She felt like a complete idiot.

As she had reached the building that housed John's company, Raytech, she had told herself it was time to come down from the clouds and plant her feet firmly on solid ground. She would put to rest her hopes and fruitless expectations of ever having any type of personal relationship with John Zachary. It had sounded sensible and practical.

And then she had been handed John's daughter.

Now the elevator doors opened on the third floor, and she stepped out. Straightening her spine and lifting her chin, she rapped on the door that had Richard Simpson's brass nameplate affixed at eye level. She had some explaining to do. She hoped John hadn't carried through with his threatened phone call to her department head. It wouldn't help. Besides, she could make her own excuses.

Ten minutes later she sat at her desk, her ears still burning from the blast of hot air from her supervisor. After a long-winded harangue, he had finally accepted her promise to stay past her normal work hours to make up the two hours she had missed. It would mean she would be leaving for the cottage later than she usually did on Fridays, but that couldn't be helped.

She pulled a contract in front of her. Before she could begin to concentrate on the figures, her phone rang. She answered it by saying her name, expecting a normal business call.

John Zachary didn't waste time with polite conversation. "Mac, come to my office."

Lauren opened her mouth to ask why, but the line went dead. "I think he means now," she mumbled as she slowly hung up the phone.

She shoved her chair back from the desk, sighing deeply. It looked as if she would have to tack on even more time to make up later.

When she arrived back at the executive office on the top floor, John's secretary ushered her into his office immediately. John was seated behind his desk, and a tearful Amy was sitting on the couch. As soon as Lauren entered, Amy ran toward her. The little girl was crying silently, tears running down her cheeks. Lauren automatically picked her up and held her close to comfort her, wondering what the problem was.

She raised her eyes to meet John's gaze and mouthed the words, "What's wrong?"

He shook his head. "I don't know," he said quietly. "All she'll say is she wants 'Lorn.' She obviously feels some sort of security with you."

Something in his voice made her ask bluntly, "Does that bother you?"

His gaze held hers, a strange expression in the depths of his dark eyes. "I can understand why she feels that way."

Lauren stared at him until her attention was claimed by Amy. The little girl raised her head from Lauren's shoulder and crooked her finger, gesturing that she wanted to tell her something. Lauren listened as Amy whispered into her ear.

She looked back at John, smiling faintly. "Amy needs to . . . ah, powder her nose."

He indicated a door on the other side of the large office. "She can use my private bathroom."

Lauren suppressed the urge to laugh. She had been summoned to take the boss's daughter to the potty. Well, she reasoned, he paid her salary. As far as she knew, her job description did not include child care, but if he wanted her to take his daughter to the bathroom, then that's what she would do.

She set Amy onto her feet, then held the girl's hand as she walked over to the door John had indicated. Before entering the bathroom, she looked back at him. He hadn't moved. His gaze remained on her and his daughter, his expression as unreadable as blank slate. She ushered Amy into the room and closed the door.

John stared at the door for a long time. His fingers thrummed impatiently on his desk. Last week if anyone had told him he was missing something vital in his life, he would have laughed. He thought he had everything. He had made a success of his electronics firm. He lived in Virginia Beach in a large condominium that faced the Atlantic Ocean. He had a number of friends, and there were plenty of willing women available when he was in the mood for female companionship. He didn't think there was a single thing he needed that he didn't already have.

That was before Amy arrived.

She had been a baby when he had divorced Martine. His ex-wife had moved to California with their only child, and he had seen Amy just twice in all that time. The excuse he gave his ex-wife and himself was he was too busy running his business to fly to the West Coast to see Amy. In a way it had been true. Since his divorce he had put all his energy into his work, needing to create some kind of success in his life after the failure of his marriage. He had found a satisfaction in his business he hadn't found anywhere else.

When he felt guilty about ignoring his only child, he would rationalize his neglect by telling himself it would simply confuse Amy to see him. Sometimes he even believed that.

He had made a number of mistakes in his lifetime. Marrying a woman who was more concerned about her appearance than anything else was one he wouldn't make again. And ignoring his child was an even more serious error, which he was not going to repeat.

Amy treated him like the stranger he was. Somehow he had to change her attitude toward him. After seeing how she reacted to Lauren McLean, he thought he might have found a way to do that.

On the other side of the door, Lauren looked around the executive bathroom. The fixtures were black, the walls white. A large mirror in a black frame hung over the sink and was the only decoration on the walls. There were no personal objects on the black marble counter beside the sink. Black-and-white towels were folded and stacked on one end of the counter. She wondered if John saw the world that way—black-and-white.

Amy could manage on her own, so Lauren walked over to the sink. As she washed her hands, she thought about John Zachary and his daughter. With its usual efficiency, the office grapevine had spread the word that he had become a full-time father three days ago. The details were a bit hazy, as much of the gossip about John was, but curiosity was at full pitch. It had been widely known he was divorced, but the grapevine had obviously slipped up about his having a child. The active rumor mill was making up for lost time with the news of his sudden fatherhood.

Lauren studied her reflection in the mirror as she wondered what type of woman attracted John Zachary. She was naturally curious about his ex-wife. After all, she was the woman he had married . . . and divorced.

Shaking her head in irritation, she frowned. You big dummy, she scolded her image silently. What difference could it possibly make what kind of woman John preferred? For the past year he hadn't shown the slightest interest in her. There was no reason that should change now.

Shadows of regret haunted her eyes, and she blinked several times to erase them. It would be more sensible to stick with her dreams. Reality was a trifle more complicated.

Amy joined her at the sink but couldn't reach the faucet. Lauren turned the water on, then lifted Amy up by her waist so she could wash her hands. She received a polite thank-you when she handed the little girl a towel to dry her hands.

When the child looked up at her, Lauren noticed Amy's cheeks seemed unusually flushed. "Do you feel all right, sugar?"

Amy nodded, her head lowered as though she were looking at her shoes.

Lauren folded the towel. Her heart went out to the little girl. She understood the confusion Amy was experiencing and could sympathize with the child. She could remember the times she had been passed from one parent to the other like a used library book. At least she had been in her teens and could halfway understand what was going on. Amy was only three. At her age she should be excited by life, chattering away a mile a minute, asking questions, curious about every little thing she saw. Instead Amy was solemn and serious with a guarded expression in her eyes.

"Are you ready to go back to your daddy's office?"

"Can we make more airplanes?" Amy asked hesitantly.

"I have to get back to my job, Amy. Remember I told you about the numbers on papers?"

"Contracts?"

"Contracts. Well, there is one waiting on my desk right now, and if I don't get it finished by a certain time, I won't be doing my job. Let's go join your daddy."

"Can I come with you?" The little girl's voice was quiet but held a trace of emotion. "I'll be very good."

Unable to resist the child's need for comfort, Lauren knelt down and took Amy in her arms, holding her close. "I know you would be good, Amy, but you must stay with your daddy."

After a moment Lauren released Amy and held out her hand. Amy obediently left the bathroom. Without even glancing at her father, she let go of Lauren's hand and crawled up onto the couch. She didn't look at either of the adults as she sat with her hands clasped in her lap.

Lauren felt torn between wanting to ease the little girl's depression and her own need to stay uninvolved. She turned and started toward the door, but John called her back. "Mac?"

With her hand on the doorknob, she looked at him over her shoulder. "Yes?"

John didn't want her to leave but couldn't order her to stay. What was it about her that had him groping for reasons to keep her in his office, he wondered.

Irritated with her apparent desire to get away from him quickly, he spoke more coolly than he intended. "I want to thank you for helping Amy. If Simpson gives you any problems about being away from your office, let me know."

Though she had no intention of doing any such thing, Lauren nodded and left his office.

Less than thirty minutes later, her phone rang again. This time she could hear Amy crying in the background as John once more ordered her to return to his office.

Mrs. Murray indicated she should go right in when Lauren entered the outer office for the third time that day. As soon as she opened the door Amy threw herself at her. The little girl was crying so hard Lauren was afraid she would make herself sick. She sat down on the couch with Amy on her lap, holding her and rocking her in an attempt to calm her. She didn't try to ask the little girl what was wrong. She concentrated on soothing her.

When she glanced up at one point, she saw John standing several feet away, his expression unreadable as he looked down at her and his daughter. He had removed his suit jacket and loosened his tie, and the sleeves of his shirt had been turned back several times. He seemed to have taken off his mantle of authority along with his suit jacket.

Gradually Amy's crying was reduced to little shuddering sobs as she clung tightly to Lauren. Through the material of her dress, Lauren could feel the heat from Amy's cheek pressed against her chest. She continued to rock the child, and the small body began to relax against her. As the minutes passed, her arms grew cramped from holding Amy, but she didn't change her position.

After what seemed like hours but was actually only five minutes, she heard John say quietly, "I think she's asleep."

Lauren eased Amy down onto the couch. She lightly touched the backs of her fingers to the little girl's cheek and forehead. "She's awfully warm, Mr. Zachary. She should be watched in case it's more than being upset."

She got up off the couch and started toward the door.

"Where are you going?" he asked.

"Back to my office."

"Not yet." This time he wasn't going to let her go. He stepped over to his desk and reached for the phone. "Mrs. Murray, will you get Richard Simpson for me, please?"

Lauren walked over to stand in front of his desk. "I've already talked to my supervisor, Mr. Zachary. Mr. Simpson has agreed to let me make up the time I've missed."

John was momentarily fascinated by the flare of anger in her eyes. "I'm going to tell Simpson you won't be back to your office the rest of the afternoon."

She didn't want him to interfere, even though he had a right to do whatever he wanted to. It *was* his company. Her voice was softly furious as she asked, "Why would you want to do that?"

His glance slid to Amy, asleep on the couch. "There's something I want to discuss with you. It might take some time."

The call had been put through, and John spoke to her supervisor, telling Simpson that he needed Lauren McLean's services for the rest of the afternoon. If Simpson had any objections, John didn't give him the opportunity to air them. He hung up the phone as soon as he was through speaking.

Pushing back his chair, he stood up. Indicating a chair in front of his desk, he said, "Why don't you sit down?"

She shook her head. "No thanks. I really don't have much time, Mr. Zachary. I have a lot of work to do."

His dark eyes drilled into her. "You work for me,

remember? I don't want to pull rank, but I will if I have to. I need to talk to you about Amy."

Lauren watched him as he raised his hand to rub the back of his neck. She got the impression he wasn't finding it easy to involve her in his personal business. That was only fair. She wasn't all that comfortable with the thought herself. It would be smarter to distance herself from John than to become embroiled in his problems.

"I only met Amy a few hours ago, Mr. Zachary. All I know about her is she is three years old and is your daughter. I don't see how I can be any help to you."

He took several long strides over to her. He looked down at her, his expression serious. "I want you to come home with me tonight."

Two

Lauren stared at him. "Excuse me?"

"With Mrs. Hamish gone, I'm on my own with Amy. I was hoping you could come to my apartment after work and help me with her. I'm new at being a father, and frankly I'm not very good at it. I could use your help."

"Mr. Zachary," she began patiently. "I'm a contract clerk. An unmarried contract clerk with no children. Why do you think I'm an expert on children?"

His quiet voice had an edge of frustration. "You've been able to reach her in only a few hours. Something I haven't been able to do in three days. I've bought her a roomful of toys, but she ignores them. You showed her how to make airplanes out of paper, and she was having a great time."

"Most children are amused by simple things, especially if by doing them they receive attention."

There was an implied criticism in her voice, but he didn't take offense. "I've tried. During the last three days, I really have tried to talk to her, to play with her. I just can't reach her. But you can. You have. In only a few hours." He walked away from her to stand in front of the window. Staring out at Norfolk's skyline, he said, "I can handle multi-million-dollar transactions, but a three-year-old child has me stumped."

Lauren looked at his profile as he continued to gaze out the window. "What do you want from me?" she asked simply.

"My daughter and I are strangers. Somehow I have to change that. You could help me. Forget you work for me. This has nothing to do with your job at Raytech. Tell me what you would do in my place."

"There are tons of books with all the advice you need on bringing up children. There are doctors and child specialists, and people experienced as parents who could advise you. I'm not qualified to hand out suggestions on how you should bring up your daughter."

"I don't have time to wait for an appointment with a child specialist. With Mrs. Hamish gone, I'm on my own right now. I have a stack of books I bought the day after Amy arrived. Reading them hasn't given me the insight, the instincts you have. I've seen what you can do with Amy. That's all the credentials you need."

She studied him a long time. The temptation to do as he asked was strong. So was the desire to get to know him better. Finally she spoke. "Could I ask you something?"

He nodded. "Ask me whatever you want."

She bit her lip as she debated whether or not to say what was on her mind. There was a fine line between giving advice and butting into someone's personal life.

John watched her. Her expressive eyes clearly

showed her doubts and apprehensions. He knew he was putting her on the spot, but he was desperate. This woman had made contact with his daughter and might be able to help him in doing the same.

When she didn't immediately say anything, he prodded, "What is it you want to know?"

She frowned, "What I want to ask you is very personal and not really any of my business."

"I'm making it your business. If it will help me with my daughter, you can ask me anything you want."

The possibilities were endless, but she narrowed the field of her questions to concentrate on his request. "Am I correct in assuming your daughter has been living with your ex-wife?"

He nodded.

"When your ex-wife brought Amy to you, was she antagonistic toward you in front of Amy? The reason I ask is if Amy heard her comments, she could be affected by her mother's attitude toward you."

His voice was hard as he replied. "Amy came by herself. My ex-wife put her on an airplane in San Francisco. I didn't even know she was arriving until I received a phone call from my ex-wife an hour before Amy's plane landed." He glanced at his sleeping daughter. "When I met her flight, she had a tag pinned on her dress as though she were a package."

When his attention shifted back to her, Lauren detected the anger in his eyes. She also noticed the way his hands tightened into fists. She had no way of knowing if his anger was directed at his ex-wife or the arrival of his daughter.

"Has your ex-wife remarried?"

He shook his head, his fingers unclenching. "When she called to notify me that Amy was coming, she told me she was involved with someone. I got the impression Amy was in the way."

Even though she was curious about the woman he had married, Lauren didn't pursue the subject other than to ask, "How long have you been divorced?"

"Over two and a half years."

"How did Amy react to you when you visited her during that time?"

It was obvious by his clipped tone, he didn't care for that particular question. "I haven't seen her as much as I should have."

She knew she was treading into sensitive territory. "It isn't uncommon for one or both divorced parents to communicate bitterness and anger to their children."

"I have no idea what Martine has told Amy about me. All I know is she's obviously afraid of me."

"Perhaps it's simply that Amy's reaction to you comes from her not having had much exposure to men in general. You're a man, and you're a stranger. It's not really so surprising she isn't comfortable with you."

He walked over to his desk and placed his palms flat on top of it. Then he leaned forward. "There's not much I can do about being a man. Do you have any suggestions how I can change the second part?"

She wished she hadn't started this, but since she had, she might as well finish it. "I know it sounds trite, but it's going to take time. You've only had Amy for three days. Give her a chance to get to know you, to become more used to you. Don't push her or try to force her to respond to you. It would help if you could be adaptable to situations as they come up."

"Adaptable?" he repeated skeptically.

She smiled. "How about flexible or spontaneous

then?" Her smile faded. "Sorry. I don't mean to be facetious. I know it's not funny. This type of situation is hard enough for older children who can understand what's going on. It has to be particularly confusing to Amy since she's so young."

John straightened as he studied her closely. "Are you speaking from personal experience or just guessing?"

Lauren rarely talked about her past, but telling him of her own adolescence might help him understand Amy's behavior. "My mother has been married four times. I was shuttled back and forth between my father and my mother from when I was fourteen until I was eighteen and went away to college. I've had three stepfathers and one stepmother and various stepbrothers and stepsisters. My brother lived with my father, so I only saw him when I was sent to my father's house. I can understand a little of how Amy is feeling. Every time I went to my father's, I was the visitor who didn't really belong. Then when I returned to my mother's home, it took me a while to adjust to her ways again. I remember feeling like a Ping-Pong ball, bouncing back and forth between two opponents, occasionally out-of-bounds, and wondering if I was ever going to make any points with either of my parents."

John walked around the desk and stopped in front of her. He placed his hands on her shoulders, a gesture that surprised them both. "Before I knew about your childhood, I asked for your help. Nothing you've said has changed my mind. In fact, you're better qualified than anyone else I know. I'm asking a lot of you, but I'm desperate. With my housekeeper gone, I'll have sole charge of Amy this weekend. I'd like you to spend some time with us, to be a buffer between Amy and me. She's comfortable with you, and she isn't with me. Maybe by watching you with her, I can learn how to relate to her."

Her heart was racing. His touch sent spirals of heat through her, confusing her. She wanted to help, not just for his sake but for Amy's as well. Still, something held her back.

When she didn't answer, his fingers tightened. "I'll make it worth your while, Mac. You name the figure and it's yours. If you want a promotion, you've got it. I don't expect you to do this for nothing."

She jerked away from him, taking several steps back. She had to keep her voice low so she wouldn't wake Amy, but her anger was obvious in her eyes and her stiff stance.

"How dare you offer me money? I would never take money from you except in my paycheck, which I earn. If I get a promotion, it will be because I deserve it, not because I've done a favor for the boss."

"I didn't mean to insult you, Mac. It's only fair you're compensated for your time." He added cynically, "I haven't met a woman yet who would do something for nothing. I wouldn't expect it, and you shouldn't offer it."

Feeling she had overreacted, Lauren reined in her temper. "If I agree—which at this moment is a very big if—it will be because I want to, not because I'm being paid."

Without knowing why, John felt it necessary to clarify his position. Watching her carefully, he said, "If you do agree to help with Amy, I would want it on a strictly business basis. That's why I offered you payment for your time. I wouldn't want you to get the wrong idea. I want you for my daughter, not for myself. I have enough complications right now. I don't need any more."

In Lauren's opinion he was digging himself into a

deeper hole. She took a deep breath and counted to ten in order to keep her temper in check. It worked. She managed to keep her voice low and controlled. "Whether or not I agree to help you with Amy, becoming personally involved with you is the last thing I want or expect. I have an unwritten rule about people I work with or for. I keep my private and professional lives separate. You'll be safe from me."

Even though she was saying what he thought he wanted to hear, John was irritated that she was agreeing with him. Slowly he stepped closer to her. Anger smoldered in her eyes, and he was fascinated by the spirit he saw, although she tried to suppress it.

"Let's see how safe I'll be," he murmured.

He gripped her shoulders and pulled her against him. She gasped in surprise, and he covered her open mouth with his. At first she held herself stiff as his firm lips moved on hers. Then she sighed into his mouth, her head whirling with a myriad of involuntary sensations. Her hands came up to his shoulders, her fingers clutching the material of his shirt. Even in her most vivid dreams she hadn't imagined the powerful rush of pleasure coursing through her. Her response was automatic when he slanted his mouth over hers, deepening the delicious assault on her senses.

John brought her body closer to his as he felt her go limp in his arms. The feel of her breasts against his chest tightened the coiling need inside him. He had meant the kiss to be an experiment, maybe even a punishment, but his intentions had changed the moment he felt her lips under his. Desire splintered through him when his tongue rasped over hers, leaving him wanting more of her. He was in danger of forgetting everything but the woman in his arms who tasted as sweet as rich warm honey.

His phone rang, an unwelcome intrusion. Its strident tone pierced the cloud of sensuality surrounding them, bringing them back to reality. On the second ring John loosened his hold on her, looking down at her for a long moment. He had shown how possible it was for them to be involved, not just to her but to himself as well.

He frowned. He couldn't believe he had let the kiss go so far. Some men took advantage of their positions as employers to gain sexual favors, but he wasn't one of them.

The phone rang again and he released her abruptly. He walked over to the phone and picked it up. "Yes?" After a brief pause, he said crisply, "Put him on."

Lauren reached for the back of the chair closest to her, shaken and off balance. It wasn't necessary to be able to read minds to know John regretted the last few minutes. She had seen his grim expression when he looked down at her. She didn't regret what had happened between them, but apparently he did.

Considering his reaction, she was surprised to realize she was going to agree to help him with his daughter. It was probably one of the dumbest things she could do, but she would be smarter on her next birthday. She could tell herself she was doing it for Amy. It would be true. Partly.

She was still reaching for that elusive apple at the top of the tree.

When John finally hung up the phone, he stayed at the desk rather than going near Lauren. He felt raw and edgy and he knew why. The problem was he couldn't do anything about it.

"I have a few phone calls to make, then I'd like to take you to dinner. Unless you have other plans." He wasn't sure why he felt it necessary to add, "Amy would be going with us, of course."

Lauren ignored the warning bells going off in her mind. "I'll have dinner with you and Amy on one condition."

"What's that?"

"That you call me by my name instead of Mac."

Suddenly he smiled. "All right, Lauren. That's easy enough. You've got a deal. As long as you call me John instead of Mr. Zachary."

Lauren felt the impact of his rare smile down to her toes. She had a sinking feeling she had just made a bargain with her conscience. It was yet to be seen whether she had made a wise one.

She returned to her office to finish up a few loose ends, having agreed to meet John and Amy in the lobby at five. She kept telling herself all she had agreed to was dinner with John and Amy. That was all. It was relatively harmless. Nothing to get excited about. If only she could get the butterflies in her stomach to believe it, she would feel a bit more relaxed.

A few minutes after five, Lauren tidied up her desk and took her purse out of a desk drawer. She was pushing back her chair when her door opened. John stood in the doorway.

She noticed he was wearing his suit jacket, and his tie was again in place. He looked like her employer once more, which made her wonder if that was the impression he wanted to give.

Thinking she must have misunderstood their earlier arrangements, she asked, "Am I late?"

He shook his head as he came into her office. "No. I'm expecting an important phone call from the West Coast and it hasn't come yet. I didn't want you standing in the lobby waiting."

He glanced around her office. Plants in attractive pottery containers sat on a long credenza in front of the window, and a few prints decorated the walls. A poster hanging behind her desk caught his attention. It was a whimsical colored cartoon of a turtle. Cobwebs connected the turtle to a tree. Printed underneath was the caption: "Make haste slowly."

A corner of his mouth curved upward as he brought his gaze back to Lauren. "Words to live by?"

"I tend to rush into things without thinking," she replied with a degree of mockery. Considering her latest decision, she thought that was an understatement.

His gaze held hers. "Following your instincts sometimes works better than analyzing and agonizing over every decision."

"Is that what you do in business? Follow your instincts?"

"It's worked so far, and not just in business transactions." He paused, then said, "Why don't you come up to my office? It might be some time before I get the call from California."

She shook her head. "I need to catch up on some work. I told Mr. Simpson I would stay later since I took a long lunch hour."

John half-sat on the corner of her desk near her chair. "I told Simpson you were doing something for me. Since I sign his paycheck, he was smart enough not to argue with me."

She smiled. "Is that your way of telling me I shouldn't argue with you either?"

All he had to do, John thought, was move his hand a few inches and he could touch her. "Would it do any good?"

"Probably not."

He was so close, she thought. Too close. His thigh

was only inches from her hand resting on the arm of her chair.

"I didn't think so."

"Did it ever occur to you how Mr. Simpson might have interpreted your statement about my doing something for you?"

John shrugged. "There isn't anything I can do to control what people think."

"The trouble is the things people think are sometimes the things people say."

"Afraid of being linked with the boss on the office grapevine?" he asked, amused.

"I wouldn't say afraid." Lauren gathered up some of the papers on her desk and stuck them in a folder. "I'd say I wasn't very excited about being the latest juicy tidbit of gossip around the water cooler."

John slid off the desk and started walking toward the door. He had to or he'd do something incredibly stupid, like pull her into his arms. "I wouldn't worry about it. Are you coming?"

She gave him a look of irritation. Unfortunately his back was turned and he didn't see it. It was easy for him to tell her not to worry about office gossip. It wouldn't touch him in his ivory tower.

She rummaged around in the middle drawer of her desk and finally found what she was looking for, a package of peanut butter crackers. "Amy is probably hungry. These will tide her over until we have dinner."

John didn't tell her the crackers weren't going to be necessary. He didn't want to ruin the surprise. He was hoping to show her just how adaptable he could be.

Several heads turned and a few eyebrows rose when her co-workers saw her leaving her office with John Zachary. Luckily Richard Simpson wasn't one of them. She knew it was a vain hope that those who saw her with John would forget about it over the weekend. Being the subject of conversation didn't appeal to her, but there was nothing she could do about it now.

As they walked to the elevator, John ignored the stares of his employees. His attention was totally on the woman at his side. Her scent drifted around him as they rode up in the elevator together. It was an elusive fragrance, flowery yet spicy, uniquely her own.

He dropped his hand from her arm before he could give in to the temptation to embrace her, kiss her. Under different circumstances, he wouldn't have hesitated to follow up on his attraction to a woman. Right now, though, he needed Lauren for Amy, not for himself. Besides, she worked for him. She wasn't any more comfortable with that fact than he was.

He leaned back against the wall of the elevator. "Why didn't you have any plans for tonight?"

She turned to meet his gaze. "Because it's my birthday?"

"That and because you're an attractive woman. And it's Friday night, the end of a workweek. Three good reasons for going out on the town."

"I was going out of town, not out on the town. I still plan to leave Norfolk for the weekend. I'll leave later than I'd planned, that's all."

He knew he didn't have any right to ask about her plans, except that he had been responsible for her changing them. "Where are you going?"

"My brother has a cottage at Kill Devil Hills in North Carolina. Danny's in the Navy, stationed at the Naval Station here in Norfolk, and is currently out at sea. His wife is expecting their first child and decided to stay with her family while Danny is gone.

They asked me to keep an eye on the cottage for them, and I go there every weekend."

"What about your parents?"

"My mother lives in Hawaii. My father has never been able to keep track of birthdays, so I don't expect to hear from him. My mother phoned me last night to wish me a happy birthday and to warn me a package was on the way." She smiled at his puzzled expression at her choice of words. "Last year my mother sent me a dozen fresh pineapples. The year before I received six orchids. I can't help wondering what delicacy she'll send me this year."

The elevator doors opened and John followed Lauren into the corridor. Mrs. Murray had stayed with Amy, who had awakened before John went to Lauren's office. As soon as he returned, she gathered up her purse and prepared to leave.

"Have you taken care of those arrangements?" John asked her.

The older woman nodded, smiling briefly at Lauren and Amy. "There were no difficulties."

"Good. Thank you, Mrs. Murray. Have a good weekend."

She acknowledged his remarks with another nod and politely said good-bye to Amy and Lauren.

Fully awake now, Amy sat next to Lauren on the couch. Confiscating more paper from John, Lauren drew funny cartoon animals, much to the delight of his daughter. When she ran out of animals, she turned the page over and printed Amy's name at the top. She put the paper down on the low coffee table and handed the pencil to Amy.

"Let's see how many times you can write your name."

Amy got down on her knees and concentrated on

copying the sample Lauren had written. When she finished, she held up the paper for Lauren to see.

The A was sideways, the M lopsided, and the Y twice the size of the other two letters. Smiling broadly, Lauren exclaimed, "That's terrific, Amy. Go show your daddy how well you write your name."

Grasping the paper tightly in her small hand, Amy got to her feet and walked around the desk. She held out the paper to John, a shy expectant look on her face.

He took the paper and studied it carefully. Then he smiled. "That's very good, Amy." He turned the paper over and looked at the comical drawings Lauren had made. Pointing to one of the sketches, he asked Amy, "What is this?"

She moved closer in order to see which one he meant. "That's a dog."

"And this one?"

"That's a cat, Daddy." She sounded a trifle disgusted that he couldn't tell what kind of creature it was.

It was the first time his daughter had called him Daddy. John's gaze lifted to meet Lauren's. She was smiling. He brought his attention back to his daughter. "So it is, Amy."

The phone on his desk rang, and he reached over to answer it. Thinking it was the important business call he was waiting for, Lauren beckoned to Amy to come away from the desk. "Show me how you write your name again."

After John hung up the phone, he said, "I'll be back in a minute."

Lauren stared at the open doorway after he had left. Then she shrugged and went back to watching Amy print her name.

Amy had managed to write her name three more

times when Lauren heard the outer door open and close. It was Amy who first saw what her father was carrying. She clapped her hands excitedly, and Lauren glanced up. Her eyes widened in astonishment.

John was carrying a tray with three large cupcakes on it, a small candle in each one. He had taken the time to light the candles before he entered his office, and they created a yellow glow on the front of his immaculate white shirt.

He set the cakes down on the coffee table in front of her. "Happy birthday, Lauren. Make a wish."

It took Lauren a minute to get over the shock. She stared at the three cupcakes for a long time, then said, "Help me blow out the candles, Amy."

When the small flames were extinguished, Lauren looked up at John. "I don't know what to say."

"I don't imagine that happens often," he said with a glint of amusement in his eyes. His gaze slid to Amy, who was eyeing the cakes, then back to Lauren, who was running her finger along the frosting on one of the cupcakes. He watched as she licked the dab of icing off her finger. The sight of her lips closing around her finger sent molten heat moving through him.

"The cakes are for dessert, not the main course," he said. There was a roughness to his voice.

He went back into the outer office and returned carrying a plastic shopping bag. He set it down on the coffee table, then removed his suit coat and loosened his tie. Lauren had to slide over on the couch when he unexpectedly sat down beside her. If she hadn't, he would have practically sat in her lap. She was speechless as he began to pull food from the bag. A hamburger was set down in front of Amy, along with french fries. Lauren's sandwich was next.

She opened the wrapping and lifted the top slice

of rye bread. "How did you know I liked Reuben sandwiches?"

"Lucky guess."

For beverages he took out cans of soft drinks for each of them. There were small paper plates and plastic forks, too, and he placed those by the cakes.

The improvised birthday celebration was the last thing Lauren had expected. "This is wonderful. How did you manage all this in such a short time?"

"When I knew dinner was going to be delayed, I made a phone call to the coffee shop downstairs. Mrs. Murray called a bakery to order a cake, but they didn't have anything but these cupcakes on hand. The security guard went to pick them up. The phone call was from him telling me the cakes and sandwiches were ready."

Lauren gazed at the impromptu meal and birthday cakes, deeply touched that he had gone to such trouble to make it a special occasion. She turned and met his dark eyes. "Thank you."

"You're welcome. I'm trying to learn to be more 'adaptable.' "

She smiled, remembering her earlier comment. "You learn quickly."

Glancing at his daughter, he saw she hadn't unwrapped her hamburger. "Amy, aren't you going to eat?"

"We're supposed to wash our hands before we eat," she said in a prim voice.

Lauren laughed. "You're absolutely right, Amy." She looked at John, amusement glittering in her eyes. "We're getting a lesson in proper etiquette from a three-year-old."

They all went into the executive bathroom and washed their hands. Amy didn't object when it was John who lifted her up so she could reach the soap and water. After she dried her hands, she returned to the table and unwrapped her hamburger. John again chose to sit beside Lauren on the couch. While they ate, Lauren asked Amy what kinds of food she liked besides hamburgers.

John listened to Amy's responses, realizing why Lauren had asked the question. He mentally made a note of Amy's preferences, although most of them seemed to be in the dessert category. When she mentioned chocolate cake for the third time, he looked at Lauren and found her smiling at him.

Usually Lauren didn't have trouble eating food of any kind. For her it was one of life's major pleasures. Tonight, however, her sandwich could have been made of cardboard for all the attention she gave it. She was too conscious of the man sitting next to her. His thigh was lightly pressing against hers, and his arm brushed hers occasionally when he reached for the french fries.

She tried to concentrate on Amy. She couldn't help noticing how careful she was with the hamburger. The little girl constantly wiped her hands, and she dabbed at her mouth with the napkin after every bite. Lauren had never seen a child so careful about staying clean. After only a couple of bites, Amy set the hamburger back down on the paper wrapping. Lauren's eyes narrowed as she examined Amy's flushed cheeks.

She was about to voice her suspicions to John when his phone rang. He put down his half-eaten sandwich and went to answer it.

Amy yawned several times and rubbed her eyes. Lauren glanced at her watch. It was only seven o'clock, yet the little girl was obviously tired, despite her nap. She took Amy's hand and led her into the bathroom. While she ran water into the sink, she laid her hand on Amy's forehead long enough to determine that her skin was exceptionally warm. Lauren knew from experience with her younger stepsisters and stepbrothers that little children could become ill very quickly. She hoped this wasn't one of those times.

"Amy, do you feel all right?"

The little girl looked at Lauren but didn't answer.

She tried again. "You know you could tell me if your tummy hurt or if you felt sick."

Amy nodded but still didn't say anything.

Lauren wrung out a washcloth and wiped Amy's face with the cool cloth. She would just have to watch the little girl closely.

She dried Amy's face and hands before gently leading her back into John's office. "Why don't you lie down for a little while, Amy?"

"I'm not sleepy," Amy said petulantly.

Lauren smiled. It was the usual protest from every child she had ever known, including herself. "Of course not. You don't even have to close your eyes. Just rest while your daddy's on the phone."

Within a few minutes, Amy was asleep.

Fifteen minutes later, John finished his conversation with the company representative in Los Angeles. He hung up the phone, then closed a file and tossed it onto a corner of his desk. He glanced at the couch. Amy was sound asleep and Lauren was writing on some of his office stationery.

He continued to watch Lauren for a few seconds. There was something both restful and stirring about her. She seemed content to sit quietly, not needing to have every ounce of his attention directed at her. She possessed a serenity he didn't realize he appreciated in a woman until he saw it in her. His body reacted to the simplest gesture she made, his desire strengthening every time he was with her. He didn't understand the attraction, but he was certainly aware of it.

He rose from his chair and walked around the desk. Since Amy took up half of the couch, there wasn't room for him. He sat down in one of the leather chairs near it.

Lauren didn't look up from what she was doing. "Was the phone call worth waiting for?"

"The Status Brothers have accepted our bid to supply the electronic system components for their new factory. Fraser Status managed to convince his brothers that converting to a mechanized assembly line will save money and be more efficient. The problem came in getting Fraser to sit still long enough to talk to him about the contract."

She looked up. "I remember him. He's about six feet seven and looks anorexic. He paced up and down the conference room as if he were walking on hot coals."

John chuckled. "You have a unique way of describing people. It makes me wonder how you'd describe me."

A faint smile touched her mouth. "I think this is as good a time as any to change the subject."

"Coward," he drawled.

"Through and through."

She set the paper she had been writing on onto the table. He glanced at it. Sketches of vases in various shapes, some with unusual designs drawn on them, covered it.

He reached over and picked up the paper. "What's this?"

She plucked the paper out of his hands. "Just doodles." She crumpled the paper, then stood up and threw it into the wastebasket beside his desk. "I really must go. I have a long drive ahead of me."

"Is someone waiting for you?"

She had been reaching for her purse. Something in his voice made her drop her hand and look at him. "No. Why?"

"I thought you might have arranged to meet someone there." When she looked surprised, he added, "It's not unheard-of for an attractive woman to share her weekends with a man, you know."

"Well I don't," she said coolly, pleased that he thought her attractive but uncomfortable about discussing her private life.

"Good," he said with obvious satisfaction. "Then Amy and I won't be in the way."

She blinked. "In the way of what?"

"You offered to help with Amy, remember?"

"I didn't realize you meant for the whole weekend. I thought you were talking about today."

Amy was disturbed by Lauren's raised voice and stirred in her sleep. John leaned forward, keeping his voice low. "Lauren, she won't even let me know when she has to go to the bathroom. You saw how upset she was earlier today when she was left alone with me. How am I going to take care of her all weekend alone?"

"I've watched you with her this evening. She showed you the drawings and let you pick her up at the sink. I don't think she's as afraid of you as you think."

John stood up and took her hand. He drew her to the other side of the room so they wouldn't disturb Amy's sleep, then gripped her upper arms to keep her in front of him.

"She was more relaxed because you were here. I agree I was able to get closer to her than before, but

I still believe it's due to the fact you were with us. She seems to find some sort of security with you. Give us this weekend, Lauren. On Monday I'll find someone to take care of her during the day, but the next two days could make a big difference in our relationship."

Lauren met his serious gaze. Desire to protect herself battled with the riotous sensations caused by his touch and his nearness. She knew he wanted her to be with him only because of his daughter and not because he was interested in her personally. As long as she didn't expect anything more of the arrangement, she wouldn't feel hurt when he no longer needed her.

He tightened his hold on her. "Lauren, I need you. Give me the next two days. Please."

It would be wonderful if he really did need her, she thought. But he wanted her only as a buffer between him and his child. She would be a complete fool to go along with his wishes, she told herself.

Having come to that conclusion, she was surprised to hear herself say, "All right. I'll do what I can to help you and Amy, but only for this weekend."

He pulled her against him and lowered his head. "You won't regret it."

His lips slanted over her parted mouth, and he drank his fill of her like a man who had been dying of thirst. Leaning against the wall behind him, he pulled her against him, his arms tightening around her slender body.

When he broke away from her mouth to taste the delicate skin below her ear, she made soft yearning sounds deep in her throat. Through the delicious haze of desire, she realized she was in danger of giving in to the needs of her body. She brought her hands up to his chest to push him away before she lost what few remnants of sense she had left.

Relinquishing his hold enough to see her face, he asked huskily, "Why?"

Considering her response to his kiss, she thought he had a right to ask that question. She met his gaze. "You wanted our association to be on a business level, remember? This doesn't feel like business to me."

He moved his hands down to her waist and then over her hips, pressing her lower body into his. He watched her eyes darken with arousal as she felt the pressure of his hard body against the juncture of her thighs.

"This doesn't feel like business to me either."

A hot surge of desire rushed through Lauren. She knew he hadn't planned this. She doubted he had expected this physical attraction any more than she had. What she didn't know was how he felt about what was happening between them.

She soon found out.

"Dammit! What in hell am I doing?"

He gripped her arms and stared down at her. Her lips were moist from his, her body trembling under his hands. He gently pushed her away. Needing more space between them, he walked to his desk and sat down heavily in his chair.

"That won't happen again," he said quietly.

Feeling dazed, Lauren smiled faintly, shaking her head.

"What's so damn funny?" he growled.

"I just thought what a shame it was that I lost my mind on my twenty-ninth birthday."

He watched her intently. "You're still going to help me?" he murmured in surprise.

"I find it hard to believe myself." She glanced at

her watch. "It takes two hours to drive to Kill Devil Hills, so we'd better get going. My bag is in my car so I don't need to go to my apartment, but you and Amy will need some clothes. Nothing fancy. The cottage is pretty informal."

He sat forward in his chair, his arms resting on the desk. "I won't take advantage of the situation, Lauren," he said seriously. "I do need your help with Amy. That's all I'll expect from you."

"I'll do what I can. That's all you can expect from me."

The rules had been set down. It remained to be seen whether either of them could abide by them.

Three

Lauren had to rouse Amy before they could leave. When she did, she discovered the little girl felt even warmer than before. Amy was fretful and cranky, and Lauren didn't think it was only because she had been abruptly awakened. Her suspicions were confirmed when Amy lifted her hand and rubbed her left ear with her fist.

She pressed her cheek against Amy's and raised her gaze to John's. "You might not be going to North Carolina after all."

"Why?" He watched as Lauren touched Amy's cheeks and forehead with the backs of her fingers. Then he sat down beside them, his gaze on his daughter. "What's wrong?"

"Amy has a fever, and she might have an ear infection."

He touched Amy's forehead. "Is that serious?"

"Not if we get her some antibiotics. Do you have a pediatrician we can call?"

"No, but there's an emergency clinic not far from my apartment. Will that do?"

She nodded. "I think it's a precaution you should take. It could be nothing, but it's better to find out for sure with children."

Amy rode with Lauren as she drove her car back to her apartment rather than leaving it in the parking garage all weekend. John followed, and they transferred her bag from her trunk to his.

Luckily the clinic wasn't busy. Lauren held Amy on her lap and played "Itsy-Bitsy Spider" with the little girl, showing her how to move her hands to the simple song. John was silent as he sat beside them on one of the uncomfortable plastic chairs in the waiting room. Ignoring the blaring television and the much-read magazines, he watched Lauren with Amy.

When it was Amy's turn to be seen, Lauren was surprised that John came with them into the examination room. He stood out of the way while the nurse took Amy's temperature. Then a woman with a stethoscope around her neck entered the room.

Lauren had been correct. Amy had an ear infection, though not a severe one. Her temperature was only a bit above normal.

The doctor took it for granted that Lauren was Amy's mother and asked if the little girl was allergic to penicillin. Lauren didn't know. When she turned to John, he wasn't able to answer either. The doctor gave Amy an antibiotic injection and several prescriptions. Just as they were ready to leave the examining room, John asked the doctor if it would harm Amy to go to North Carolina for the weekend. The doctor didn't see any problems with Amy taking the trip, as long as she didn't go swimming, took her medication, and got plenty of rest.

John then asked if the doctor could recommend a pediatrician. She wrote down a name on a blank prescription form and handed it to him.

As they walked to the car Lauren said, "I should have driven my own car. Then you wouldn't have to take me back home."

John put his hand on her arm, forcing her to stop walking. "What are you talking about? Why do you have to go home? Your bag is in my car."

"We were going to the cottage before we learned Amy was ill."

He loosened his grip, although he didn't release her. "And we're still going to the cottage. You heard the doctor. It won't hurt Amy to make the trip." He looked at his daughter, who was holding onto Lauren's hand. "How about it, Amy? Do you feel like taking a ride in the car or would you rather go home to bed?"

"I want to go with Lorn."

His gaze returned to Lauren. A corner of his mouth slanted upward. "We want to go with Lorn," he said, mimicking Amy's pronunciation.

He could see her battling with a decision, and he asked, "If we stayed in town, would you stay with us?"

She shook her head. "I have to go to the cottage. I promised Danny I would water the plants every weekend and check to make sure everything is all right."

He came up with another argument. "Which is better for Amy? An apartment where she would be stuck with a man who is a stranger to her, or a cottage with someone she trusts?"

Lauren made a last feeble attempt. "It's a two-hour drive."

"I don't mind driving at night."

"All right," she said with resignation. "Just don't expect too much."

Relief washed over him. He slid his hand down her arm to lace his fingers through hers, surprising them both with the intimate twining of their hands.

Their eyes locked for a brief electric moment, both of them aware of the attraction swirling around them. The air seemed to shift and crackle as though a storm were imminent.

Lauren was the first to look away, when Amy became impatient and tugged at her other hand. As she walked toward the car with John on one side of her and Amy on the other, she wasn't aware of how her fingers tightened around the two hands she held.

The prescriptions were filled at a nearby drugstore. When John returned to the car, he slid behind the wheel but didn't immediately start the engine. He glanced over his shoulder at his daughter, who was sleeping soundly on the back seat. Amy had taken the suit coat he had tossed into the back after leaving the clinic and had made a pillow of it.

"Do you think she's warm enough?" he asked Lauren in a low voice.

She answered with a question. "Are you?"

He brought his gaze to meet hers. "I'm concerned about her comfort, not mine," he said with an edge of irritation.

"You took off your suit coat because you were too warm. If you become cool, you'll put it back on. When you do, put a sweater on Amy. If it's raining, you would wear a raincoat. Amy would get just as wet as you, so put one on her too. If it's snowing, you would put on a pair of boots and a heavier coat. Do the same for Amy."

His mouth curved into a slight smile. "You make it sound so simple."

She shook her head. "I never said it was going to be easy, Mr. Zachary."

He frowned again. "John."

She went on, correcting her use of his name. "John,

being responsible for a child is one of the hardest jobs in the world. It's trial and error, with mistakes on the parent's side as well as on the child's. You're going to make mistakes, but so will she. All you can do is take one day at a time, using common sense and your instincts. That's true of any relationship." She tilted her head to one side. "You have a jump on the situation, whether you realize it or not."

"What do you mean?"

"You care. You can't get that out of books or from me. Either you do or you don't. And you do."

"Caring about her didn't help when the doctor asked if she was allergic to penicillin. It made me realize how much I have to learn about her. Martine should have sent her medical records with her."

"Maybe she didn't think Amy would be with you long enough to need them."

He handed her the bag containing the medicine, then reached forward to start the engine. "Well, she's wrong."

Lauren stared at him, wondering what he meant. She could have asked, but she didn't. She was there because of his daughter, not to quiz him about his relationship with his ex-wife.

They were both silent as he drove along Shore Drive. Eventually he parked in front of the imposing entrance to a large white building. It was stark and modern, built in tiers that faced the ocean. Since Amy was still asleep, Lauren stayed in the car with her while John went up to his apartment to pack some things for himself and his daughter.

Lauren used the time alone to mull over the unusual events of the day. The speed with which she had become involved with John Zachary and his child was amazing, but she didn't regret her decision to help. At least not yet. She couldn't have done anything else. Part of her compliance to John's request had come from her sympathy for Amy's situation. Perhaps Amy sensed Lauren's empathy and responded to it. Whatever the reason, Lauren was enmeshed in John's life, at least temporarily.

She looked toward the entrance of his apartment building as he strode through the doors. There was enough illumination for her to see he had changed clothes and was carrying a single canvas carryall in one hand. It was the first time she had seen him casually dressed. She felt her heartbeat accelerate as he approached her, aware of his lithe grace. Snug jeans hugged his slim hips, and a cream-colored cotton pullover accentuated his dark hair and tanned skin.

He placed his bag in the trunk, then joined her in the front seat. After a quick glance at his sleeping daughter, he looked at her.

It was odd, she thought, how the atmosphere suddenly became charged with energy as their eyes met. Only a small space separated them, and she found it difficult to breathe normally.

John's arm came up to rest on back of the seat, his hand almost touching her hair. "How many excuses have you come up with for me to take you home?"

She smiled weakly. "About a dozen."

His fingers teased the ends of her hair. "I thought so. I know this whole situation is strange, but I'm not going to apologize for pushing you into it. I'll do whatever I have to to make Amy happy."

Which included using her, Lauren reminded herself. She turned her head and he had to drop his hand from her hair. "Then we'd better get started."

John felt something shift deep inside him. Was it disappointment he heard in her voice, he wondered.

Was it disappointment he was feeling as well? What had he wanted to hear her say? That she understood? He already knew that. If she didn't understand his predicament, she wouldn't be there.

So why did he feel he was missing something vital? he asked himself as he started the car. Maybe he would discover what it was during their weekend together.

John didn't need directions until they passed the Wright Brothers Memorial in Kill Devil Hills. He turned off the highway, away from the ocean, and followed the gently curving road, his headlights dancing over the blacktop. Small cottages with boats alongside could be briefly seen nestled in clumps of trees.

Seeing the size of the cottages made him ask her about the one they were heading for. "I didn't think before. How big is this cottage of your brother's?"

She kept her gaze on the road ahead. "Big enough, Mr. Zachary. You won't be uncomfortable. Turn left at the next corner."

His fingers tightened on the wheel. He was sorely tempted to pull over to the side of the road, except there was no shoulder. If she called him Mr. Zachary one more time, though, he would stop the car no matter where they were.

Following her directions, he turned off the road onto a gravel lane. Trees and shrubs lined the narrow drive, ending in a clearing. As he slowed the car the headlights picked out a large log cabin at the end of the road. It was a two-story dwelling complete with double garage and several outbuildings located near the main house. Moonlight shimmered over the rippling surface of water on the other side of the log building. The cabin was on the shore of Collington Harbor, a stretch of water off Albemarle Sound.

Lauren opened her purse and took out a small rectangular object. She aimed it toward the cabin and pressed it. One of the garage doors began to rise and exterior lights attached to the cottage came on, illuminating the drive and surrounding area.

"So much for roughing it," John murmured. "I didn't realize the Navy paid so well."

"The cottage was built by my sister-in-law's father. After Sheila's mother died, he never used it but didn't have the heart to sell it. He gave it to Danny and Sheila for a wedding present."

"Isn't it a rather long commute between here and Norfolk?"

"Sheila stayed here during the week, and Danny would come down every weekend. There's plenty of room in the garage if you want to park your car in there rather than leave it outside."

John drove inside and shut off the engine. While he got their luggage out of the trunk, Lauren went inside to turn on the lights. She ran up the stairs and quickly made up a single bed in one of the spare rooms for Amy.

She heard John calling her name. "I'm up here. Second room on the right."

Thirty minutes later, Amy was tucked into bed and their luggage had been placed in the various bedrooms. Lauren had made a pot of coffee and was standing on the porch facing the water, drinking from a pottery mug. She had changed her clothes, shedding the faster pace of the city as she had removed her dress. The jeans she had tugged on were soft and almost white with age and numerous washings, fitting her like a glove. She wore a red-and-white striped sleeveless cropped top that barely reached the waistband of her jeans.

The screen door creaked as John came outside. He was holding a mug of coffee that matched hers.

"I can see why you like to come here," he said as he stood beside her.

Still staring out at the water, she murmured, "Sometimes, especially if I'm tired, I almost talk myself out of making the long drive down here. I never regret it once I'm here."

His gaze shifted from the view of the Currituck Sound to her face illuminated by the moonlight. "I can see why. This place and you have a lot in common."

She turned her head to look at him. "In what way?"

He took a sip of coffee, his gaze never leaving her face. "It's private," he said, lowering the mug. "So are you. The trees and shrubs that surround the cottage act as a shield for things outsiders shouldn't see. To some extent I suppose we all camouflage ourselves in one way or another. The surface of the water has hidden depths. So do you."

She half-turned toward him, setting her empty mug on the porch railing. "You think you know me so well after only one day?"

Her hair was being tousled gently by the wind, and several silky strands brushed across her cheek. His hand tightened around his mug to keep from reaching out to touch her. "I don't know you as well as I will eventually."

She felt oddly threatened, although he hadn't moved toward her. Her pride wouldn't let her back away from him. She lifted her chin. "You expect a lot from a weekend."

Her face was in shadow now. He couldn't see her expression clearly, but he could hear the wariness in her voice. He was going too fast, and he knew it. Yet his body was telling him he wasn't moving fast enough.

Resting his hip against the railing, he asked, "Speaking of this weekend, what's on the agenda for tomorrow?"

"Shopping."

"Shopping? I drove for two hours so we could go shopping?"

She picked up her mug. "It'll only take an hour, maybe less. Amy needs a pair of shorts and a cool top to play in. When I unpacked her clothes, I saw all you packed for her were two fancy dresses."

"That's all she's got. My ex-wife apparently wanted to create Amy in her own image."

Lauren thought she heard amusement in his tone. "Does your ex-wife also have a thing about being clean? I've noticed Amy has a fetish for avoiding dirt."

"Martine wages war against dirt, dust, untidiness, disorder. She's like a delicate piece of ornamental glass, lovely to look at but not meant to be handled."

He had just told her a great deal about his marriage, she mused. Perhaps more than he had intended.

"Well," she said, "for this weekend Amy's going to act like a three-year-old little girl. It will help if she looks like one. The clothes will be a start."

Telling herself she wasn't running away, she took a step toward the door. "I'm going to go check on her. She was a little restless when I put her to bed."

His voice halted her. "Lauren?"

She hesitated, her hand on the half-opened door. Then she looked at him. "Yes?"

He moved slowly toward her, stopping a foot away. He lifted his hand and placed it on the door, just above hers. "I haven't thanked you for what you're doing for me and Amy."

"Why don't you wait until the weekend is over to thank me? I haven't done anything yet."

"You've given up your weekend." He gave in to the need to touch her, letting his knuckles trail down the delicate lines of her face. "What would you be doing if we weren't here?"

The evening air was cool, but she felt hot. The feel of his flesh on hers sent desire filtering through her skin to her nerve endings. She cleared her throat, hoping her voice wouldn't betray her.

"Nothing very exciting. Watering plants, dusting furniture, that sort of thing. You might end up being bored out of your mind."

Touching her wasn't enough. John dropped his hand and walked back to the railing. "I may go out of my mind, but it won't be from boredom." He turned his back to her and looked out over the water. "Good night, Lauren."

She stared at him for a long moment, then went inside, shutting the screen door softly behind her.

A foreign sound penetrated his sleep and woke John. He rolled onto his stomach and fumbled for the clock on his nightstand, puzzled when his hand didn't find it in its usual place. His eyes felt gritty from lack of sleep as he dragged them open. The first thing he saw was a painting on the opposite wall. It depicted an Indian woman kneeling on the ground putting grains of corn into a decorated clay pot. On the floor beneath the painting was a large ceramic pot that exactly matched the one in front of the Indian woman.

He should have expected pottery in the bedroom, he thought. Why should the bedroom be spared? There were pots in various sizes throughout the whole cottage, even in the bathroom. He has stubbed his toe on one and had nearly knocked another off a table when he had come into the cottage after taking a walk before going to bed. Lauren's sister-in-law apparently had a thing about pottery.

The tantalizing fragrance of coffee drifted under the door, giving him the incentive to get out of bed. As he tossed back the covers, he heard the soft murmur of feminine voices, one his daughter's and the other belonging to the woman who was the reason he had had trouble falling asleep.

Ten minutes later John entered the kitchen, stopping abruptly just inside the doorway. Amy, at least he thought it was Amy, was standing on a stool next to the table stirring something in a large bowl. Gone were the fancy dress, patent leather shoes, and braids. She was wearing an oversize T-shirt with a large yellow Happy Face on the front. And that was all. Her hair had been combed and tied into a ponytail.

He looked for Lauren and found her standing in front of the stove with a spatula in her hand. She was wearing white shorts and another cropped top, this one beige with white dots. It was her shapely bare legs that held his attention the longest. Her face was devoid of makeup, her shiny blond hair falling onto her cheek as she bent her head over the skillet. Then she reached across the stove to pick up a saltshaker, and he saw the expanse of skin above her waist. He wanted to slide his hand over her flesh, tracing the slender curves of her body. A surge of desire jolted through him, and he looked away.

He needed a cup of coffee.

Amy noticed him first. "Hi, Daddy. I'm making pancakes."

He walked over to the table and looked into the bowl. Attempting to enter into the spirit of things, he asked, "What are those blue things?"

"Blueberries. Lorn said they make the best pancakes."

Lauren turned her head and met his gaze. She read him perfectly. She knew a desperate man when she saw one. "The coffeepot is next to the sink."

"I'm in your debt," he muttered, trying not to sound as grumpy as he felt.

By the time he was on his second cup of coffee, Lauren had prepared the pancakes, fried sausages, fixed scrambled eggs, and set the table with Amy's help. She had defrosted the carton of milk she'd left in the freezer last weekend and now poured a glass for Amy and invited her guests to sit down. Before Amy sat, Lauren stacked two phone books on her chair to give the little girl added height.

John asked how Amy was this morning, and Lauren told him the little girl's fever was gone. Amy nodded. "Lorn said I can go outside, but I still have to take my medicine."

While they ate Lauren outlined her suggestions for the day. "We can dash into town and buy a few things for Amy. Then we can go for a walk in the woods, go fishing, walk on the beach, and catch crabs for dinner."

"You don't have a beach," Amy said.

Lauren smiled at her. "The Atlantic Ocean does. It's not that far away. We can take our shoes off and walk in the sand, build a sand castle, and feed the sea gulls." She looked at John. "How does that sound?"

"Exhausting."

She heard the dry humor in his voice and responded to it. "You'll have to keep up with us girls or we'll leave you behind."

He usually didn't bother with breakfast, so he was surprised to find himself reaching for another pancake. "I can handle the walk in the woods and on the beach, but I'm a little shaky about the catching crabs part. I've eaten crabs, but I've never caught one in my life. It sounds potentially painful."

She passed him the syrup. "It won't hurt a bit."

"How about the shopping?"

She grinned. "It might damage your checkbook a little, but other than that, you might even enjoy it."

He wouldn't have used the word enjoy to describe the experience of shopping with his daughter and Lauren. It was certainly interesting and different. Lauren made a game of the simple task of picking out and trying on clothes. If it had been up to him, he would have left the choice of clothes for Amy to a salesclerk. That wasn't Lauren's way. She got Amy actively involved in choosing her own outfits, tactfully eliminating some questionable styles and color combinations.

When she stopped after two outfits, John asked Lauren to select at least a dozen more. She hesitated, and he started pulling pieces of clothing off the racks and holding them up for Amy. When he held up a lacy white garment, he saw Lauren smile broadly and heard Amy giggle.

He looked from one to the other. "What's so funny?"

"That happens to be a slip. It's worn under a dress, not instead of one."

He held up the item on the hanger to examine it closer. "So it is."

Lauren took it from him and hung it back on the rack. "I would have thought you would know the difference no matter what size it might be."

Amusement flickered in his eyes. "Maybe I'm not the man of the world you think I am."

She had to admit he had a point. He had been full of surprises in many ways. "Apparently not. You didn't think this shopping trip would be so educational, did you?"

"I'm learning something every minute." He retired to a chair and sat down. "I'll leave the rest of the shopping to you two experts."

The frilly dress Amy had worn to the shopping center was folded and tucked away into a bag. At Lauren's suggestion, Amy wore one of her new outfits out of the store. John carried the numerous bags they had accumulated, although Lauren offered to help tote the purchases.

"One of us has to have a hand free to buy the ice cream," he said.

Amy looked up at him expectantly. "Ice cream? Can we have some ice cream?"

"Sure. What kind would you like?"

"Nilla with sprinkles."

He blinked, then looked at Lauren for a translation. She supplied it. "Vanilla ice cream with bits of colored candy sprinkled on top."

He didn't think it sounded particularly appetizing, but if that was what Amy wanted, that's what she would get.

They found a place to buy the ice cream and sat at an outside table with a spectacular view of the ocean. John drank a cup of coffee while Lauren and Amy dipped into their dishes of ice cream. Amy had gotten her wish and happily spooned off the tiny multicolored bits of candy before digging into the mass of vanilla. Lauren had ordered a gooey confection of lime sherbet covered with chocolate and topped with whipped cream.

Catching his slightly horrified expression as she brought the spoon up to her mouth, she grinned and happily ate the sherbet. She was unaware of how the sight of her pink tongue sliding over her bottom lip affected him. She dipped the spoon into her dish and held it out to him.

"Want a taste?"

His gaze remained fixed on her mouth, and his voice was blatantly suggestive as he said, "Not of the ice cream."

"That's all I'm offering," she said casually, surprised her voice wasn't as flimsy as her defenses against him.

He raised his eyes to meet hers. "Is it?"

"Yes." It was odd how hard it was to say one simple word. Probably because it was the biggest lie she had told in a long time.

Amy had followed the conversation between the two adults, her eyes shifting back and forth as though she were watching a tennis match. The warm July sun was beating down on them, melting the ice cream at a fast rate. Because she wasn't paying attention to what she was doing, a dollop of ice cream fell off her spoon onto the front of her new top.

She made a small sound of dismay and looked up at her father with wide, frightened eyes.

John saw the fear in her eyes and wondered why it was there. Spilling a little ice cream didn't seem a major catastrophe to him, but apparently it was to her.

His instincts told him to deal with the situation as lightly as possible. He handed her a napkin. "Here, kitten. Mop up and finish your ice cream before the sea gulls decide to eat it for you."

She took the napkin and wiped at her top, her hand shaking. "I didn't mean to. It just fell off."

"Accidents happen, Amy," he said quietly. "Don't worry about it. Your clothes will wash."

John saw the concern in Lauren's eyes as she

watched Amy rubbing frantically at the spot on her front. Then she did something that totally surprised him. While Amy was concentrating on removing the offending ice cream, Lauren stuck her spoon into her dish and purposely let a bit of lime green sherbet and chocolate syrup fall onto her own top.

"You'd better pass me the napkin when you're done with it, Amy," she said casually. "Look what I just did."

The little girl's eyes widened as she saw the stain on Lauren's top. Then she glanced at her father to see what his reaction was.

Aware of his daughter's attention on him, John handed Lauren another napkin. "I'm going to have to get some more napkins if you two keep this up," he said with amusement.

Lauren smiled at Amy. "He's just cranky because he ordered dull old coffee instead of nummy ice cream."

"My dull old coffee is all gone, and Amy's ice cream is turning into nilla soup. If you're going to finish that glop, you'd better hurry."

Amy stared at him. "Aren't you mad? I'm all messy."

"A little messy never hurt anyone, kitten. That's what soap and water are for."

Lauren grinned. "The way we're going, we'll have to trot down to the ocean and get cleaned up before we get into your car."

Amy's expression was full of wonder and delight. She looked at the waves easing up onto the sandy beach, then back at Lauren. "Could we go closer to the water?"

"We can even go in the water. At least our feet can. Take your shoes off, and we'll walk on the beach. Maybe we can find a seashell or two."

John watched Lauren and Amy remove their sandals as he mulled over the last few minutes. With Lauren's help the incident of the spilled ice cream had been smoothed over. Later he would make a point of discussing Amy's reaction with Lauren. He could tell her why he felt Amy was so paranoid about staying clean, but he wasn't sure how to go about changing it.

He looked up. Lauren was standing by the table with her hands on her hips, looking impatient. "What?"

"Your shoes," she said, pointing at his leather loafers.

"What about them?"

"You're still wearing them."

He liked the way her eyes sparkled with life and laughter. "You're very observant."

As though she were talking to a rather dense rock, she said slowly, "If you don't take them off, they'll get wet."

"Why? Is it going to rain?"

After a few seconds of staring at him with narrowed eyes, Lauren bent down and whispered in Amy's ear. When she straightened up, she went around one side of the table while Amy went around the other. They each took one of his hands and tugged him to his feet.

"Ganging up on me? Is that fair?"

They pulled him toward the beach. "It's two against one," Lauren said. "Majority rules."

"A mere male doesn't stand a chance then." He took their hands. "Never let it be said I was a poor sport. If it's a walk on the beach you want, that's what you'll get." He paused to remove his shoes and socks and roll up his pant legs. "The doctor said Amy wasn't to go swimming."

"She isn't going swimming, just wading. It's over

ninety degrees today, and she won't get chilled. She's had her medicine, and we'll watch her carefully."

It was Amy's plea that convinced him. "Come on, Daddy."

As they dodged the waves and let the seawater wash over their feet, Amy held onto his hand. He heard her laughter and excitement, her soiled clothing forgotten, at least for the moment. She brought tiny shells for them to see, showing them to him as freely as she did to Lauren.

For the first time since she had arrived at the airport, he felt there was hope for a closer relationship with his daughter.

At one point Lauren accidentally brushed up against him as she dodged a larger than usual wave. He felt the tantalizing curve of her hip and her soft breast on his arm. Such a simple thing, a mere grazing touch, and he was shaken to the core.

He planned to become better acquainted with Lauren McLean along with his daughter before the weekend was over.

Four

Lauren insisted on Amy's having a nap in the afternoon. She gave her the medication and tucked her into her bed. The child didn't have a fever any longer, but Lauren preferred to be overcautious rather than the least bit careless with Amy's health. The sunshine, sea air, and exercise had tired her enough for her to go to sleep without much protest.

While Lauren was upstairs with Amy, John was in the spacious living room examining an unusual piece of pottery. He ran his fingers over its rough surface, his thoughts on the events of the morning.

Strolling on the beach wasn't usually his scene. Assisting Lauren with preparing lunch wasn't something he would have imagined himself doing either. He went to restaurants or ate takeout food. He didn't heat up tomato soup, much less eat the soup with a toasted cheese sandwich. He didn't dry dishes or wipe milk off a little girl's face.

But he had done all those things. And had enjoyed them.

All morning Lauren had found reasons for Amy to talk to him, to show him what she had found, encouraging the child to ask her father questions about various objects on the beach. Her strategy, if that's what it was, had worked. Amy approached him more freely, even taking his hand voluntarily as they strolled on the beach. He wasn't foolish enough to think all their problems were solved after only one morning. There was still a long way to go, but it was not as far as it had seemed yesterday.

Even though her bare feet made no sound on the pine floor, he knew that Lauren had entered the room. His stomach tightened as the awareness of her stabbed through him. He set the vase down and slowly turned.

He had seen and been with women more beautiful than she. So why did his heart suddenly race when he was near her? He had never had that response to her before. He had known her for a year without having any reactions to her beyond his usual appreciation for an attractive, intelligent woman. When had his feelings changed from casual interest to intense physical desire? And what was he going to do about it?

Unaware of the direction of his thoughts, Lauren glanced briefly at the vase he had been inspecting. "Do you like pottery, Mr. Zachary?"

"I thought we'd agreed to be on a first-name basis."

She picked up the vase. "I've been thinking about that. I don't believe it's a good idea for me to get used to calling you John, when on Monday you'll be Mr. Zachary again."

"Force yourself," he ordered bluntly. "I'm not going to be reverting to Mac on Monday or any other day."

She shrugged as if it didn't matter to her one way or the other. "You're the boss."

"Only at Raytech," he drawled. "I have a solution. If all that's stopping you from using my name is the fact that you work for me, then you're fired."

Lauren made a choking sound and started laughing. "All right, so I'm overreacting, being silly, and . . ." She stopped. "You can step in here at any time to contradict me."

"You're doing fine." He ran a finger down her nose and along her jaw. "Put up as many barriers as you want, but don't be too surprised when I knock them all down."

She was saved from answering by the sound of heavy footsteps on the porch, followed by hard knuckles striking the door. She set the vase back on the table. "That's probably Silas."

John heard a deep male voice respond to Lauren's greeting as she opened the door. As soon as she did, a shaggy bundle of fur dashed inside. The dog's breed was questionable but not his nature. His tail wagged steadily while Lauren automatically patted his head and didn't stop its constant rhythm when he came over to John.

Instead of inviting the dog's owner in, Lauren stepped outside. "What have you got for me today, Silas?"

Silas Trane shoved his calloused hands under the bib of his overalls and said in his gravelly voice, "Some good-size ones. Caught this morning. Can't get them much fresher."

Lauren could have mouthed the words along with her neighbor, since they were the same phrases he said every Saturday when he brought her crabs, shrimps, or fish. Six days a week he went out with his two sons on their fishing boat on Albemarle Sound. Previously he had brought things to Danny and Sheila, and he continued supplying Lauren with the catch of the day after her brother and sister-in-law left. His skin was like gnarled leather, tanned and tough from daily exposure to the sun and salt water. He was kind in a gruff sort of way, with a consideration for women reminiscent of Civil War times. After knowing her for over a year, she was still Miss Lauren. He still carried anything heavier than a grapefruit into the cottage for her.

She walked around the cottage beside Silas to his pickup truck. His youngest son stepped down from the cab of the truck as they approached. Tony Trane was nineteen, with enough muscles for three men. He wore a shirt that had the sleeves torn off and ragged cutoff jeans, exposing legs and arms as stout as oak trees.

He gave her his usual greeting, a bear hug. Like the dog, he was friendly and showed it. "How ya doing, Lauren?"

She gasped for breath and was relieved when he let her go. "Hi, Tony. I'm doing just fine." She walked over to the back of the truck. "I have a couple of houseguests, so I hope you brought a few extra of whatever you caught."

Silas lowered the tailgate. "Depends on how hungry they are."

She peeked into a large plastic pail. There was a thick layer of chipped ice covering whatever was in the bucket. She stuck her hand down into the ice and brought out a pink shrimp. "Thank you, Silas. I love fresh shrimp."

Silas scooped out some extra shrimp from another pail and put them into the one he had set aside for Lauren. Then he jerked his head toward the part of the porch that extended around the side of the cottage. "Is that your houseguest?"

Lauren followed the older's man gaze. John had

come outside and was leaning a shoulder against one of the posts supporting the porch roof. He was watching her.

"Yes." She introduced John to Silas and his son. "This is John Zachary, my employer. He and his daughter are spending the weekend here. Mr. Zachary, this is Silas Trane and his son, Tony. They live in the large house around the point. Silas runs a fishing boat and his two sons help him."

John came down the steps. Stopping beside Lauren, he shook hands with the two men.

"You from Norfolk too?" Silas asked.

"Yes."

"First time down here?"

"With Lauren. I've been to Nags Head several times on business."

Tony looked from Lauren to John, then back to Lauren. "Doing a little extra work over the weekend?" he murmured, raising an eyebrow. Then he grinned. "Sure beats the heck out of you spending all your time with that clay."

"I'm so glad you approve, Tony," she said dryly. She turned her attention back to the pail of shrimp. "I'd better get these inside. The ice is melting."

When Tony reached for the pail, John walked over to the back of the truck. "I'll take that."

Tony handed over the pail as though it weighed little more than a loaf of bread. John grunted and tightened his grip on the handle as he took the full weight of the pail.

Lauren thanked Silas for the shrimp, adding "Is the offer still open for me to go out with you again one of these weekends?"

"Any time you say." The older man paused, looked at John, then back at Lauren. "Will you be needing extra for next weekend?"

She shook her head and said, "No," at the same time John replied, "Yes, she will." He placed his arm around her shoulders in a possessive gesture that surprised them both.

Silas cleared his throat, a curious expression on his face. "Nora told me to remind you about the pig pickin' this afternoon, Miss Lauren. We need a good turnout so I hope you can come." Glancing at John, he added, "Your guest is welcome, too, of course."

She had forgotten all about it. "We'll try to make it. John's daughter hasn't been well. We'll have to see how she feels when she gets up from her nap."

Silas nodded and got into the truck. Tony whistled loudly and the dog came bounding around the corner of the cottage. He jumped into the back of the truck, his tail wagging steadily.

Lauren stood beside John as Tony backed the pickup down the gravel driveway. As soon as it was out of sight, she jerked away from John. "Why did you do that?" she asked angrily.

"Do what?"

"Give them the impression you're more than my employer."

He walked toward the steps, carrying the pail. "I am." He stopped and looked at her over his shoulder. "I gave the exact impression I wanted to give." She was still glaring at him. Turning, he faced her. "Lauren," he began patiently, "I didn't like that young Neanderthal touching you. Call it staking a claim if you like. Now he knows how things are."

For a few minutes it was impossible for Lauren to pull her thoughts together. Finally she said, "That's more than I know."

He glanced down into the pail. "Hadn't we better get these shrimp cleaned? They don't look like they're getting any younger."

"In a minute. I want to clear this up. You were the one who wanted this weekend to be kept on a business level only, remember? You're here because of Amy. That's the only reason."

His eyes were serious as they met hers. "I know why I'm here, Lauren. It isn't likely I'll forget."

He was being deliberately evasive. She sighed and said, "We can clean the shrimp on the porch. Why don't you check on your daughter while I get a pan?"

The cleaning of the shrimp was delayed a few minutes when John discovered Amy had awakened. She immediately asked for Lauren, so he brought her outside to the porch.

Lauren didn't ask Amy to help them. Cleaning shrimp wasn't something the little girl would find fun. With Amy disliking getting messy, taking the heads off slippery shrimp certainly wouldn't appeal to her. Lauren went into the kitchen and came back with a glass of milk and a cookie.

While she and John dismembered the shrimp, Amy sat down on the top step a little distance away, drinking her milk and munching on the cookie. She had peered into the bucket, said, "Yuk!" and left them to it. She seemed perfectly satisfied to watch the activity on the Currituck Sound—the occasional boat, the birds flying overhead.

John saw how expertly Lauren removed the heads of the shrimp, cleaning three in the time it took him to do one. She would dip her hand into the icy water up to her elbow and withdraw plump shrimp, whose heads she popped off with her thumb. Occasional splashes of water fell on her legs and shorts, and her hair blew lightly around her face.

As she reached into the plastic bucket for another shrimp, she noticed John was no longer helping her. She looked at him. He was leaning back against the wall with his arms folded over his chest. He was watching her with an odd concentration.

"What?" she asked crossly.

"I'm trying to figure you out."

She plunged her hand back into the pail. "Figure me out? You make me sound like a crossword puzzle."

"There isn't a single woman I know who could rip the heads off shrimp with such ease. You're a woman of many parts."

His phrasing amused her. Tossing a shrimp into the pan, she said lightly, "I have just as many parts as any other woman."

He didn't even want to think about her attractive parts. "I've noticed," he said dryly. "You're good with figures in the contract department, can easily charm three-year-olds, and now I discover you're an expert at decapitating seafood. It makes me wonder what's next."

"The pig pickin' is next." She dried her hands on the towel across her lap. "That is if you want to go. If you don't, perhaps you and Amy can go for a walk in the woods behind the cottage. You could show her flowers and plants, things like that."

"I'd rather we all went to the pig pickin', whatever that is. That's the purpose of this weekend, isn't it? Being together."

She handed him the towel. "The purpose of this weekend is for you to get to know your daughter. You can do without me for a couple of hours."

"I could, but I don't want to." A muscle in his jaw clenched and his eyes hardened. "Would you rather go without us? Is that what you're trying to tell me?"

"No, that's not what I'm saying." She glanced over at Amy, then looked back at him. "After this week-end is over, you're going to have her all to yourself.

This afternoon would be as good a time as any for you to be alone with her."

His dark eyes searched hers. She was very wary of him, more than the occasion called for, and he couldn't help wondering why. He was getting tired of taking one step toward her only to have her take two steps away from him. There had to be a reason for her behavior. It was up to him to find out what it was.

But the time wasn't right. "Tell me about the pig pickin'."

"I guess they don't have pig pickin' in New Hampshire."

"How do you know I'm from New Hampshire?"

"The Raytech grapevine." She smiled when his eyes widened in surprise. "You have to expect your employees to be curious about the man who signs their paychecks."

"No I don't. My private life is none of their business or anyone else's. What else have you heard about me?"

She paused for a moment as she gathered her information. "You're an only child. Your mother is living in a retirement community in Florida. Your father passed away when you were in college. You play racquetball every Tuesday and Thursday. You contribute to charities but not to politicians. The grapevine knew you were divorced but wasn't aware you had a child. You've been approached by a large conglomerate that wants to buy your company, but you've turned them down. That's about it."

He looked thoroughly bemused, but not angry. "What's my shoe size?"

She smiled. "Sorry. That information wasn't available."

He tilted his head to one side. "The grapevine is

why you didn't like people looking at us yesterday when we left your office, isn't it?"

Her smile faded. "The people who saw us won't know our being together was as innocent as it was. They'll have a field day creating a situation that doesn't exist."

Considering that his thoughts at the time hadn't been so innocent, John couldn't blame the staff for thinking what they obviously did. Then he realized the position he had inadvertently put her in. If any of his staff knew they were spending the weekend together, her reputation would be in shreds. Even though they hadn't been intimate, that was not how the majority of people would see it. They would automatically think he and Lauren were having an affair. There were names for women who slept with the boss, and none of them were nice.

"If anyone gives you a hard time, will you tell me?"

"Probably not." She saw him frown. "We were seen together in the hall. That's all. There's nothing for anyone to talk about, so don't worry about it."

He didn't pursue it any further. "You were going to tell me about the pig pickin'."

She handed him the towel. "A pig pickin' is where everyone eats a roast pig and tons of other food and generally has a good old time. There's a small fee for this particular pig roast to raise money for the upkeep of the cemetery that's across the street from where the pig pickin' is held."

He wiped his hands. "Sounds like fun. When do we leave?"

She picked up the pan of cleaned shrimp. "In about two hours. What would you like to do until then?"

"What would you be doing if we weren't here? You watered the plants and dusted the furniture earlier."

Her smile was slightly enigmatic. "I doubt if you would enjoy what I usually do."

"Why don't you try me? I'm even game to go crabbing."

She studied him for a long moment. "I usually work."

That was the last thing he thought she would say. His expression reflected his surprise. "Work? What kind of work? Unless Simpson has started a program of doling out extra work I don't know about, you don't have anything to do for Raytech."

"It's not that kind of work."

"Now you have me curious, Lauren."

She considered whether or not to show him how she spent her weekends. Making up her mind, she called to Amy. "We're going for a little walk. You want to come with us?"

Instead of heading down toward the water to go crabbing or fishing or taking a walk in the woods, Lauren led the way to one of the small outbuildings behind the cottage. Before opening the door, she asked Amy not to touch anything unless she asked first.

Amy nodded and Lauren unlocked the door. A potter's wheel stood in the middle of the room. On two walls were shelves containing clay pots, cups, goblets, mugs, and vases in a variety of sizes, shapes, and glazes. A small kiln was set on firebricks in one corner. A low square table next to the potter's wheel held modeling tools, all neatly lined up and ready for use. Two smocks hung from a peg by the door.

John stared. "This is what you do every weekend? All that pottery in the cottage and in your office is yours?"

She shook her head. "Most of it is Sheila's. I'm only learning. She said I could use her equipment while she's gone, and I do."

He walked over to one of the shelf units where a number of finished pots were displayed. "You're full of surprises."

"Why? Because I'm learning to make pottery?"

"That's part of it."

She felt oddly defensive without knowing why. "What's the rest of it?"

He turned away from the shelf and faced her. "This cottage, the pottery, your weekend. It's all so solitary. I would have thought you would be spending time with friends."

"You mean you thought I would be with a man?"

"It's not unheard of. Women do it all the time."

"So do men." She glanced at Amy who was idly pushing the wheel around with her hand. "You do realize there are going to be changes in your lifestyle now that you have a child full time."

He knew what she was implying. It was true his social life had become nonexistent since Amy had arrived. His gaze went to his daughter, then back to Lauren. The sun shining through the window picked up the highlights in her hair and outlined her slender figure. He hadn't a single regret for the way things were turning out.

"Having my daughter has its advantages. Because of Amy I've been invited to spend the weekend with a beautiful woman. I have no complaints so far."

"The weekend's not over yet. I'll take your complaints on Sunday night." She took Amy's hand and drew the little girl toward the door. "The tour of the pottery factory is over for now. How about a walk in the woods? Let's see if we can find some wild flowers to use for decoration in the cottage. Then we'll get dressed for a picnic. How does that sound?"

John didn't follow them right away. She was doing it again, he thought. Any approach he made was turned back on him like an unwanted gift. He gazed around the room, taking in all the equipment and the finished pottery. This was where she spent her spare time on weekends. Shaping clay instead of forming any kind of personal life. He wondered if he would discover this weekend why she was hiding away in North Carolina. Why was she pushing him away?

Amy came to the door. "Daddy? Aren't you coming with us?"

"I'm coming, Amy." After one last look he left the shed.

For an hour they walked in the woods, returning to the cottage with handfuls of wild flowers that they stuck in pottery vases. Then it was time to get ready for the festivities. For John it was simply a matter of changing his shirt after the tramp through the woods. Lauren took only a few minutes to remove her dusty top and shorts and slip on a pair of pink-cuffed shorts and a white scoop neck top worn under a pink-and-white shirt open down the front. A leather belt around her waist completed the outfit. It hadn't taken a great deal of time for her to select what to wear. Amy, however, wasn't finding it so easy to choose which of her new clothes to put on.

From the top of the stairs, Lauren called down to John, asking him to come upstairs. When he appeared at the doorway of Amy's bedroom, he asked, "You wanted me?"

Lauren could have made a comment, but she didn't. She wanted him more than her next breath. Wanting and having were two completely separate things. "Your daughter needs some advice. It seems she has a problem deciding what to wear."

He took in the assortment of clothes laid out on the bed. It looked like Amy had taken all the outfits they had purchased that morning and spread them out on the bed.

He looked up and met Lauren's amused gaze. "I'm supposed to help her choose? I'm the guy who thought a slip was a dress, remember?"

Lauren glanced at Amy, who had picked up a blue-striped top and an orange-dotted pair of shorts. "I doubt if you could do worse."

"I think you're right."

She headed out the door. "I'll leave you to it."

Ten minutes later John left Amy's bedroom. He and Amy had finally agreed on an outfit, although not till after an interesting hassle. He had just had another lesson in parenthood.

As he passed Lauren's bedroom, he saw her on her hands and knees peering under her bed. This time he had no problem recognizing her from the back.

He leaned against the frame of the door. "Lose something?"

She straightened up. Giving him a brief glance, she muttered, "Yes. A gold bangle bracelet. I was sure I brought it with me last weekend, but I can't find it now."

He stepped over to the dresser where an oval pottery dish was sitting at one end. Inside was a collection of costume jewelry mixed in with strands of gold and silver. Sifting through the baubles and beads and metal, he found a circlet of gold. "Is this it?"

She walked over to him. "Thanks. Would you believe I looked through all of that and didn't see it?"

"At this moment I'll believe anything." He saw the way she fingered the bracelet after sliding it onto her wrist. "That seems to be important to you."

She dropped her hand from the bracelet. "I keep

telling myself not to get attached to things. I left it here on purpose to prove I could manage just fine without it. Is Amy ready? We should be leaving soon."

"She informed me she could get dressed by herself." He wanted to get back to Lauren's previous comment. "Why do you feel you have to do without the bracelet? Obviously you're fond of it."

"That's why."

"You've lost me. I don't understand."

"It doesn't pay to become attached to things. It's harder when you lose them."

John's eyes narrowed as he watched her walk over to her closet. He felt as though he had been kicked in the stomach. In his mind he heard what she hadn't said. She wasn't talking only about material possessions. She didn't want to become attached to people or objects because she didn't want to be hurt when she lost them.

His gut instincts told him he had just discovered why she pushed him away every time she thought he was getting too close. She didn't want to become involved with him because she didn't expect whatever they had between them to last. From her description of her family life, all the relationships she had had growing up had been short-term. She was protecting herself in the only way she knew how.

He watched her graceful movements as she slipped her feet into sandals and fastened the small straps. She didn't know it, but he wasn't going to be lost or misplaced.

"I didn't hear any major battle coming from Amy's room," she said as she faced him. "Did you have any trouble helping her choose what to wear?"

"I didn't realize what a diplomat a parent had to be. She was so excited about all her new clothes, she wanted to wear several of them at the same time."

"How did you persuade her to wear only one outfit?"

He smiled. "I told her if she wore only one new outfit each day, she would have longer to enjoy them all."

Lauren returned his smile. "Very good. You're learning fast."

"I have a good teacher." He walked over to the bed and sat down. "She wanted me to brush her hair for her, but I told her you would help her after she changed."

Lauren bit her lip to keep from laughing. "You make it sound as though she asked you to do something horrible. Her hair has to be brushed daily, you know. You might as well get used to doing it. She's too young to do it herself."

"What do I know about brushing a little girl's hair?"

"You comb your own hair, don't you. It's the same thing."

"No it isn't. Her hair is long and fine. I might hurt her."

She went to her dresser and picked up the ivory comb and brush set Danny had given her for her sixteenth birthday. Walking over to John, she showed them to him. "These aren't instruments of torture. You won't hurt her."

He looked at them, then at her. Smiling faintly, he asked, "Do these come with a set of instructions?"

"Practice first then. It's really not that difficult."

For a moment he simply looked at the brush and comb. Then he stood up and took them from her. "What a good idea."

He nudged her until she was sitting on the bed. Surprised, she asked, "What are you doing?"

The mattress gave under his weight. "You said to practice. That's what I'm going to do."

"I meant on yourself. Not on me." She started to

get off the bed, but he pressed his hand against her shoulder to keep her where she was.

"If I'm going to practice the fine art of hair brushing, you're going to have to hold still."

He knelt close behind her. Then she felt the brush flow softly down the back of her head. His hand followed each stroking motion, his touch as soft as a gentle breeze. Instead of using the comb, he let his fingers glide through the strands of her silky hair.

Delicious sensations melted her resistance with each stroke of his fingers combing through her hair. Sighing softly, she relaxed her stiff spine and allowed herself to enjoy his touch. Her eyes closed as his fingers caressed the taut cords in her neck.

The bed shifted slightly as he moved closer until she was between his thighs. He put his hand on her shoulder and felt her tense. "Relax," he murmured.

His breath was warm against her neck, sending waves of heat along her veins. How was she supposed to relax when every nerve ending was throbbing in reaction to his touch, she wondered frantically.

She opened her eyes and saw their reflection in the mirror on the vanity. "I think you've got the hang of it now, John."

His hand tightened on the nape of her neck as she began to draw away from him. "That wasn't so difficult after all."

"I told you it wouldn't be."

"I meant saying my name."

The pressure of his fingers eased her backward until she was leaning against his chest. The brush fell onto the bedspread as he slid his arm around her waist. He felt her shudder, heard her quick intake of air. Giving in to the need to feel more of her, he spread his hand out, grazing across her rib cage up to her breasts. His fingers teased and stroked, and he reveled in the way her breast filled his hand.

Her head fell back on his shoulder. "John," she said breathlessly. "No."

He lowered his head and nuzzled her neck. "Lauren. Yes."

Shifting to one side, he applied pressure with his arm. In one smooth motion, she was on her back with his body partially covering hers.

He looked down at her, expecting a protest. Instead her eyes were glazed with arousal. A strange sense of triumph surged through him when he realized she was as caught up in the delicious desire as he was.

His mouth closed over hers with unleashed hunger. A hand at her throat kept her head still as he broke open her mouth to taste the moist warmth inside. Then his hand moved down to the curve of her shoulder, savoring the feel of her. Need became a hot, pounding rush within him, a molten passion searing his senses.

He lifted his head enough to see her face. What he saw made his breath catch. Even if he hadn't been experienced with women, he would have been able to recognize the desire glimmering in her tawny brown eyes. He wanted to crush her softness into the mattress with his hard body, delve into the seductive heat of her.

For the moment he satisfied his need by caressing her hip with his hand, then her thigh. Inserting his knee between hers, he parted her legs, making her more vulnerable to his touch. His fingers found the hem of her shorts and worked their way underneath. He pressed his mouth to hers once again, absorbing her soft moan of pleasure and helplessness as his fingers edged under the barriers of her silk panties and found the intimate warmth between her thighs.

She breathed his name and arched her hips into his hand, tossing her head back and forth as she fought the incredible sensations flowing over her.

Her name came from him like a caress against her lips. "So hot, so feminine and beautiful."

Lauren felt as though she had fallen into a whirlpool of passion. She was drowning in a sea of sensation unlike anything she had ever felt before. Somewhere in the depths of her mind, she remembered they weren't alone in the cottage.

She had to stop the magic he was creating in her while she still could. Inserting her hand between their bodies, she grasped his wrist. Her strength didn't equal his, but she said the one word that would stop him, more powerful than "no."

"Amy."

John froze. His intentions collapsed, but his need still ran thick and hot through his bloodstream. Burying his face in her neck, he took a deep, steadying breath. Even as he inhaled the fragrance of her skin, he fought for control.

After a few seconds, he rolled off her. To his surprise Lauren didn't immediately leap off the bed but remained beside him. His fingers slid sideways several inches until he found her hand. A deep husky laugh filled the silence before he murmured, "I think I need a few more lessons."

Lauren made a choking sound. "You've got to be kidding."

He propped himself up on his elbow. A small smile played around his mouth. "I meant as a father."

She wanted to trace the shape of his lips, but she didn't. "Then what kind of lessons are you talking about? You passed hair brushing."

His smile faded. "I forgot all about her, Lauren. All I had to do was feel you under me, and I didn't give a single thought to Amy. What kind of father does that make me?"

Her fingers tightened around his. "A human one." It was time, she decided, to put the last few minutes in their proper place. Somehow she was going to have to convince him it had been only a momentary thing. She didn't want him to think her response was anything serious.

"John, I—"

They both heard the sound of small sandals on the pine floor of the hall. Sitting up, Lauren looked down at John. "Seeing us on a bed together isn't one of the lessons Amy needs at this time in her life."

"It's what I need at this time in my life," he said hoarsely, but still pushed himself up and off the bed. He pulled Lauren to her feet with him and quickly kissed her. "We'll get back to this later. I believe we have a pig pickin' to attend first."

"But—"

He tugged at her hand. "No buts about it. Let's go. I can hardly wait to pick at this pig or whatever we're supposed to do."

Five

Considering the number of people attending the pig pickin', Lauren thought an hour later, the cemetery fund would be in good shape. It was a beautiful day, with clear blue skies and big appetites bringing many people to the charity affair. Food stalls were clustered at one side of the field, while various games were played a safe distance away. Several athletic young people and a few energetic older folks were throwing Frisbees, batting softballs, tossing horseshoes, and lofting badminton birdies across a net.

Having attended other gatherings like this one, Lauren wasn't surprised by anything she saw. Amy, however, took in everything as if, like a little girl named Alice, she had suddenly found herself in Wonderland. From her expression, she was both fascinated and frightened by the noise, the crowds, the laughter, and all the activity.

As they neared a stand selling homemade pies, Nora Trane greeted Lauren. Silas's wife was a motherly woman in her fifties, gregarious, with frank eyes that missed little. She was the exact opposite of her laconic husband in nature and appearance. Her love of bright colors was reflected in the colorful fuchsia shirt she wore over a pair of white slacks. Plastic replicas of fruit dangled from her ears, matching a chunky necklace that clattered with her every movement behind the stall counter.

To Nora, the world and all its occupants were there to be hugged to her generous bosom, and she now embraced Lauren. After introductions were made, Nora immediately bent down to fold Amy in her arms, exclaiming what a pretty little thing she was. Next she gave John a hug, then examined him carefully.

"Silas mentioned you had company this weekend, Lauren. I admit I was curious. You've never had a houseguest before. In fact, this is the first time you've had a man st—"

Lauren quickly interrupted her. "I'd like to buy one of your famous sweet-potato pies, Nora. I'm sure John and Amy have never tasted anything like it."

Nothing could have pleased Nora more. Two pies were placed in a long cardboard box and handed over to John. Nora would take money for only one of them, insisting the second one was free.

Grinning at Lauren, she said, "Haven't you ever heard that old saying, the way to a man's heart is through his stomach? Well, my sweet-potato pie is a guaranteed shortcut."

John tucked the box under his arm. "That must be some pie."

Nora patted his cheek. "I doubt very much if Lauren needs shortcuts to your heart."

In an attempt to put an end to Nora's provocative conversation, Lauren said, "It's good seeing you again, Nora. We need to be moving on. There are a few more things I want Amy to see."

"Of course, honey." Nora winked. "I understand perfectly. Don't forget the picnic table contest. Maybe John would like to join in."

Lauren shook her head. "I think we'll just watch. It'll be safer."

"Safer?" John asked, puzzled. "What could be dangerous about a picnic table?"

When a younger woman behind the counter of Nora's booth called to her, she said, "I gotta go. Marty needs me. Lauren, you explain about the contest." Giving John a broad smile, she added, "I hope we see you again, John. Perhaps you would like to go out on the boat with Silas one day. Lauren has been out and enjoyed it. Amy could stay at the house with me."

Before Lauren could speak, John said, "We'd like that, Mrs. Trane."

"Please call me Nora." She tilted her head to one side. "I have a feeling we'll be seeing a lot of you, John Zachary. Or am I wrong?"

John glanced briefly at Lauren, then back at Nora. "Not as far as I'm concerned."

Lauren held tightly to Amy's hand and began to walk away. This was getting out of control. Trying to stop Nora from pairing them off would be like attempting to halt an elephant by putting up a paper wall. Nora was taking it for granted John was more than a weekend guest and her employer. Like Noah, the older woman thought everybody in the world should go in twos.

When John's long stride caught him up with Lauren and Amy, he asked, "What's this about a picnic table contest?"

"People pay to pile on top of a wooden picnic table until it collapses. The record, I believe, is thirty-seven." She glanced at him. "If you really want to try it, I understand it's a great way to meet people."

He slipped his arm through hers. "I'll pass, thanks."

They did watch the contest when it took place. An old picnic table had been cordoned off by a rope fence. The crowd of onlookers stayed on the other side of the rope, giving the people lined up plenty of room. A man with a megaphone was the official counter, loudly proclaiming the total each time someone climbed onto the table, and sometimes onto other people. There was a great deal of laughing, falling off, climbing back on, and eventually, a satisfying crunch with all the participants crashing to the ground. The old record of thirty-seven was beaten by two, and there were no casualties other than a few splinters and a couple of bruised bottoms.

John had lifted Amy up in his arms so the little girl could see better. When the table collapsed, she covered her mouth, uttering a sound of distress. Then she saw that everyone was all right and relatively unscathed, and laughed and clapped as the contestants gradually unfolded from the heap of bodies.

John chuckled. "And I thought I had seen everything."

"If you enjoyed that," Lauren said, "perhaps you would like to see the balloon bashing."

"You're joking."

She laughed. "I'm serious. Balloons are filled with water and people pay money to throw bean bags at them to try to break them. It's not as easy as it sounds."

Amy wiggled with excitement in his arms. "Could we? Could we, Daddy?"

Smiling at his daughter's excited face, he said,

"Why not? Since this seems to be the weekend for new experiences, we might as well go all the way."

When he set Amy down, she reached for his hand as if it were something she did all the time. He clasped it and looked over at Lauren.

As their eyes met, his heart pounded painfully at the exquisitely gentle expression in hers. It was amazing the difference two days had made; in his daughter's attitude toward him and his toward Lauren. His fingers tightened around his daughter's hand. Then he raised his other hand, holding it out toward Lauren. She looked puzzled for a moment, then she lifted her hand and took his.

There was an odd feeling of fullness in his chest, an overwhelming tenderness crowding out every other thought and emotion. He couldn't put a name to the way he felt because he had never experienced anything like it before. Whatever it was, it felt right, the way it should be.

Amy suddenly pulled at his hand. She had to tug again to get his attention. "Daddy, I have to go."

He looked down at her. "We'll leave in a little while, Amy. I thought you wanted to bash some balloons."

"Daddy," she said plaintively. "I really have to go."

It dawned on him what his daughter meant. He looked at Lauren, who was grinning with amusement. "Does she mean what I think she means?"

She nodded. "Isn't it wonderful?"

He gave her a blank look.

"This time she told you. Isn't that what you wanted?"

It was, but now what did he do? he wondered, feeling foolish. "Do you happen to have any idea where I can take her?"

"This way." As they walked along, she said, "Lesson number one hundred and four. Whenever you arrive at a place you're not familiar with, always check out where the restrooms are. You never know when you're going to need one."

"You did that when we arrived?"

"Habit. I had to babysit a younger stepbrother a lot. Lucky for you I did."

John agreed. This father stuff was requiring expertise he had never considered before. Now he had to be constantly on the lookout for potties.

Several hours later, they had finally eaten all they wanted to eat and seen all there was to see. Amy's little feet were dragging with weariness as they walked to the car. John picked her up and carried her, ridiculously pleased when her small arms wrapped around his neck.

When they arrived at the cottage, he carried Amy to her bedroom and helped Lauren put her to bed. Once they had dressed her in her nightgown, tucked her in, and given her her medicine, she rolled onto her side, one small hand under her cheek. Her eyes closed almost immediately.

John remained beside the bed. "She looks so tiny, so defenseless," he murmured.

"She is, but she's also stronger than you might expect." She touched his arm. "Let's let her sleep. She's had a full day."

As he followed Lauren down the stairs, he admired the fluid movements of her body. "Haven't we all," he muttered.

At the bottom of the steps, she stopped and looked up at him. "I know just what you need," she said casually.

A corner of his mouth twitched. "So do I, but I don't think it's the same thing."

The only sign she gave of understanding his meaning was a fleeting glimpse of awareness in her eyes.

"Why don't you go into the living room and relax? I'll make us some coffee."

As she walked toward the kitchen, she heard him grumble, "I knew it wasn't the same thing."

Ten minutes later she joined him in the living room. John was seated on the couch with his legs stretched out in front of him and crossed at the ankles. She set the tray she was carrying down on the coffee table—a wooden lobster cage covered with thick glass.

Picking up one of the mugs, she curled her legs under her and settled back in the corner of the couch.

While they waited for the coffee to cool, they talked over the events of the day, from the shopping to the pig pickin'. Later John would look back on the evening with a measure of surprise at how long and how easily they talked. He couldn't remember any other occasion when he had enjoyed the simple pleasure of being with a woman. The sexual awareness was always just under the surface, but it was enough to talk with her, relax beside her, sharing the day they had spent together.

"Are you saving Nora's sweet-potato pie for tomorrow?" he asked as he lifted his coffee mug from the table.

"I forgot about the pies. I left the box in the back seat of your car. I'll go get it."

He flung out his arm to halt her as she uncoiled her legs. "Stay put. I don't really want any right now. I'll get the pies out of the car later."

He raised his mug and took a healthy swallow, suddenly gasping and choking. There was more than just coffee in there. He cleared his throat. "I wasn't expecting coffee with a kick in it."

"I put a drop or two of whiskey in. I thought regular coffee might keep you awake."

"I might have trouble sleeping, but it won't be from the coffee," he muttered dryly.

"Too much excitement for you today?"

"It'll be for the same reason I had trouble sleeping last night." He caught her puzzled look. "No, it isn't from an uncomfortable bed or the strange surroundings."

"Insomnia?"

"No, it's you."

She studied him for a moment, her expression serious and oddly sad. "You don't need to say things like that, John."

He shifted slightly to face her. "Even if it's true?"

"It's not true. There's nothing between us except the mutual desire to make the adjustment easier for Amy."

He set his mug down on the table. "You don't really believe that, do you?"

"I've worked for you for over a year, and I doubt if you've lost any sleep during that time because of me. Don't expect me to believe that thoughts about me are keeping you awake now."

"I hadn't kissed you then."

Uncertainty battled with desire, her heartbeat accelerating uncomfortably as her eyes locked with his. The uncertainty won. "First you tell me you want this arrangement on a strictly business level. Then you kiss me to prove we could be involved if you allowed it to happen, which you say you won't. Now you're telling me you're losing sleep because of me."

"I don't blame you for being confused. I'm having a little trouble sorting everything out too." Something changed in his eyes as he gazed at her. "To give you an example, I've always thought you didn't care much for me."

Afraid she would give herself away, she said defensively, "I didn't even know you. I still don't."

"You won't get to know me if you keep pushing me away."

She was unable to deny she was doing any such thing. "What do you want from me, John?"

"To trust me to have some staying power."

"Staying power? What are you talking about?"

He shook his head. "It doesn't matter right now. I think you're a lady who has to be shown. Time will take care of that."

She set her mug down on the table and stood up. "We have one more day here. That's all the time you have."

John came after her. She had taken only a few steps when his arm shot out to halt her. With his hand on her arm, he whirled her around, bringing her against his hard frame.

Lowering his head, he murmured, "Then I'd better not waste another minute."

His mouth covered hers, his arms crushing her against his aroused body. His hungry demand rocked her senses. As his hands began to move over her back, his tongue invaded her mouth. A shiver of response ran through her as the kiss deepened, and she was drawn into the primitive realm of passion.

He broke away from her mouth briefly. "Touch me, Lauren. I need to feel your hands on me."

As though she were a puppet and he controlled the strings, she lifted her arms to encircle his neck. Her hands grasped and stroked the firm muscles of his back. When he didn't immediately kiss her, she brought her hands to the back of his head to hold him still as she claimed his mouth.

John felt an overpowering sense of triumph. Her response delighted him, arousing a deep satisfaction within him. She wasn't pushing him away but was accompanying him on the rising spiral of passion.

His hands cupped her bottom, holding her against his demanding body. He felt her shudder and tried to hold onto his slipping control. Bringing her with him, he slowly moved back to the couch without releasing her mouth.

A soft sound of surprise came from her throat when the back of her knees hit the edge of the couch. She was gently lowered to the cushions. His weight crushed her, leaving her breathless yet more aroused than she could ever imagine being. Air in her lungs she could do without, but not this magic, this heated intensity.

When his mouth left hers, he sought the soft fragrant flesh of her neck. His knee intruded between her legs, forcing them apart. He could feel her trembling beneath him as his hard body communicated his need and desire.

Experience told him she wanted him as badly as he wanted her. No, he corrected himself. Almost as much. She couldn't possibly match the desire searing his blood. Then he raised his head and looked down at her. He had to admit he might be wrong again. The licking flames of desire were in her eyes. Molten heat emanated from her flushed skin, creating a deeper need for him to feel her flesh against his.

He had never felt this intensity that was both pleasure and pain. It was more than raw passion. It was simply more than anything he had ever imagined hunger for a woman could be.

This woman. Only her.

He brought his hands up to cup her face. Leaning on his elbows to partially take his weight off her, he murmured, "You might think this happens often between a man and a woman, but I've never had it happen so quickly or so urgently."

"John," she whispered achingly. "This isn't wise."

His thumbs stroked her jawline. "Maybe not, but I'm not strong enough to turn away from it."

"You want a woman and I'm available."

If she had hoped to anger him, she was doomed to disappointment. He saw the uncertainty in the depths of her glazed eyes. Something stirred within him, a tenderness that responded to the wariness in her. Although his body was taut and throbbing with need, he knew he wouldn't go any further.

He rolled off her completely and sat up, bringing her with him. Smoothing her mussed hair away from her face, he let his forefinger trail across her moist bottom lip. "One of these days you'll realize it's you I want and that not just any woman will do. I'll wait until then." His smile wavered a little. "Just don't take too long."

He stood up and pulled her to her feet. Placing his hands on her shoulders, he looked down at her. "For now why don't you go to bed before I forget my good intentions?"

"John," she began, her voice breathless. "I think we should talk about this."

He slipped his arm around her waist, bringing her lower body into his. Hearing her gasp and seeing her eyes glaze as she was confronted with the evidence of his desire, he murmured, "Go while I can still let you, Lauren. A few minutes more of holding you, and I won't be able to keep from making love to you. I'm trying to do the right thing. I know you aren't sure about us. I'm giving you the space you need until you are."

She held his gaze for a long moment, indecision warring with her common sense. Desire coursed through her veins and deep into the core of her, making it difficult to turn away from the one man who could make her feel so alive and desirable.

Easing out of his arms, she wondered why it felt wrong to be doing the right thing. She should be grateful he had released her from the desire binding them together. Her nerve endings were raw and sore. There was an emptiness deep inside her that ached to be filled. She couldn't appreciate his generosity at that moment. Maybe she would later.

He watched her walk toward the stairs. "Lauren?"

She didn't turn, but she did stop walking, her spine stiff as though she were preparing herself for a blow.

"I hope you don't walk in your sleep. I've used up all my good deeds for today. I can't promise to leave you alone again if I see you wandering around tonight."

She nodded slowly and went up the stairs. Several times she had to grip the railing tightly to keep from flying back down the stairs into his arms. Without once looking back, she slipped into her bedroom and quietly shut the door.

Sunlight was pouring through the window, slanting across the bed and John's pillow. Shielding his eyes with his hand, he opened them and turned his head. The small clock on the bedside table told him the time was a little after eight.

There were no sounds coming from downstairs when he opened the door after he had showered and dressed. The kitchen was empty, and he wondered where Lauren and Amy had gone. A pot of coffee waited for him on the counter next to the sink. Alongside was a plate covered in foil. Lifting an edge of the foil, he saw a couple of homemade biscuits filled with sausage patties. Taking one of them with him along with a cup of coffee, he left the kitchen and went to the front door to look out toward the water. There was no sign of either Lauren or Amy.

"Dammit," he muttered. "Where the hell are they?"

He didn't like the sudden tug of fear. Maybe he should have listened to Lauren last night when she had wanted to talk. He didn't know how she felt about what had happened between them because he hadn't allowed her to tell him. The only thing on his mind then had been his rampant desire. It had crowded out every other thought.

Shoving open the door, he walked out onto the porch. He nibbled at the sausage biscuit and drank his coffee, fighting down the urge to check to see if his car was still parked in the garage. She wouldn't have just left with Amy without telling him. He might not have known her long or well, but he knew that much about her.

He sat down and looked out over the sound while he finished the sausage biscuit and coffee. All he had to do was wait for them to come back from wherever they had gone to. That's all he had to do.

He managed to wait four minutes and twenty-two seconds. Luckily the pottery mug was sturdy and could withstand the jolt of being set forcibly down on a wooden table by a man at the end of his patience. John paced the porch several times, trying to figure out which direction he should take to try to find the two females who had disappeared.

As he passed the table for the third time, his gaze caught the coffee mug. He stopped walking and stared at it. Abruptly turning around, he headed toward the steps and took them two at a time. He strode around the corner of the cottage toward the outbuilding Lauren had shown him the day before. As he approached he saw the door open and heard his daughter chattering away a mile a minute.

Stopping in the doorway, he was able to see them, but they hadn't seen him. Lauren was sitting at the potter's wheel, and Amy was seated at a small table with a lump of clay in front of her. Lauren wore a baggy chambray shirt, shirttails tied in a knot at her waist and sleeves rolled up to her elbows, and a pair of cutoff denim shorts. Amy looked comfortable and cool in one of her new outfits, her hair tied back in a ponytail. She was fingering the clay tentatively as she talked to Lauren.

"This is so sticky and gooey, Lorn. I'm getting all dirty."

Lauren's own hands were immersed up to her wrists in clay as the base of her pot spun around. "Sometimes sticky and gooey can create beautiful things, Amy. See all the vases and cups on those shelves? They all started out like that clay in front of you. Remember the pancake batter you stirred for me yesterday? The batter was sticky and gooey, but you ate a pancake after it was cooked."

"My mommy said it's bad to get dirty," Amy said in a quiet voice. "Girls should always be neat and tidy or people won't like them."

John's jaw clenched tightly as he heard his daughter paraphrase his ex-wife. He was about to enter the shed, although he didn't know what he was going to say to Amy. Then he heard Lauren speak.

"I'm not saying your mother is wrong, Amy. Some people don't like to get dirty, and that's okay. There's nothing wrong with people wanting to be clean." Lauren stopped the wheel and held out her hands, watery clay dripping from them. "But there's nothing wrong with this either. If I get a little untidy while

I'm doing something that's important to me, I don't worry about it. This washes off when I'm through, and I have something to show for my time."

Amy poked the clay again. "Mommy said Daddy wouldn't like it if I got dirty."

Lauren searched for the right answer. She didn't have the right to interfere in the way Amy's mother was raising her. Granted, John had asked for her help with Amy, but that didn't give her carte blanche to cavalierly dispute the views of his ex-wife. Yet the child shouldn't be so preoccupied with being clean. "Your daddy didn't get angry when you spilled ice cream on your top yesterday. He knew it was an accident, just like when I got some of my ice cream on my shirt."

"Daddy doesn't get dirty."

Since prior to this weekend Lauren had never seen John in anything but immaculate suits, she had to agree with Amy. "Maybe not now that he's an adult. He's a businessman who works with his mind, not his hands. But it would be surprising if he didn't get scrungy when he was young. Most little boys play baseball, climb trees, and grub around in the dirt all the time."

She resumed spinning the potter's wheel and dipped her hands back into a pan of water at her side. While she continued shaping the clay into a pot, she told Amy about some of the escapades she and her brother had gotten into when they were young.

Amy listened with rapt attention as Lauren told her about washing a muddy English sheep dog. "How that dog hated a bath, and we had to wrestle him into the washtub." Chuckling, Lauren added, "The dog ended up clean, but Danny and I were covered in mud and soap and water."

"Did you get into trouble?"

Lauren laughed. "We got a bath."

John turned and walked back toward the porch. He went over everything Lauren had said and wondered how he could make Amy see him differently. Lauren, too, for that matter. They apparently saw him as a one-dimensional figure, a man in a business suit. That perception was as incorrect as his had been about Lauren. She had shown him parts of herself he hadn't seen before. Now it was time for him to reveal more of himself. How he was going to to do that was something he'd have to think about.

As he climbed the porch steps, he happened to notice that several weeds had stuck to the lower part of his jeans from his walking through the grass. Stopping abruptly on the third step, he picked off the weeds and threw them back onto the ground. Suddenly he looked around at the ground surrounding the cottage. He smiled. He had found his answer.

An unusual noise intruded into the shed, drowning out the sound of the potter's wheel. Lauren stopped the wheel and listened. Frowning, she grabbed a towel and wiped her hands as she walked to the door.

"What's that noise?" Amy asked.

Lauren looked out. "Your father is mowing the lawn." Her voice was slightly dazed.

She left the shed and covered the ground quickly to stand in the path of the power mower. Several feet from her John stopped and shut off the engine. He smiled faintly when he saw the signs of irritation in her eyes and around her mouth. Then her gaze flicked over his chest, exposed by his open shirt, and her expression changed. When she brought her gaze back to his face, he could see the desire, the need, in the depths of her eyes. However unwilling to admit it, she was attracted, and he found his body reacting to that knowledge.

She set her hands on her hips. "What do you think you're doing?"

Since it was obvious what he was doing, he knew she wasn't asking what but why. "I'm earning my keep."

"You don't have to do work around here. That wasn't part of the deal for the weekend."

"I know I don't have to, but I want to." He smiled. "I'm enjoying it. You might ask Amy to bring me out a cool drink later though. This is hot work."

As far as John was concerned, the conversation was over. The lawn mower roared to life, and he waited for her to move out of his way.

That wasn't the only chore John took on as the morning passed. After the weeds and grass had been mowed, he raked up the clippings and gathered other debris, like fallen branches. Even when Lauren and Amy returned to the cottage, he continued to work outside. As the sun rose higher in the sky, the temperature rose as well, and John removed his shirt, throwing it over the porch rail.

Lauren could see him from the window above the kitchen sink as she filled a large saucepan with water. His moist skin glistened in the sunlight, and the muscles in his back and arms flexed as he trimmed a bush. When the pan overflowed, she dragged her attention back to what she was doing. Turning off the water, she allowed herself one more glimpse of the man outside. He wasn't playing fair, she thought. The sight of his bare chest aroused a curious fluttering sensation in the pit of her stomach. And a throbbing heat lower in her body. Her hands ached to touch his slick skin and—

"Damn," she muttered under her breath. He was driving her crazy. The funny thing was, part of her craved these intoxicating sensations as a starving person sought food. Her mind might scream warnings at her, but her body disregarded them when he touched her. Or when he didn't touch her. All she had to do was see him, be in the same room with him, and her sensitive body would ache.

Sighing heavily, she carried the pan to the stove and turned on the burner. The attraction she had felt for him in the past was a pale memory compared to the intensity of her emotions now. She knew she was pushing him away, and so did he. The difference was she was aware of the reasons. He wasn't.

If she was being overcautious, she felt she had good reason to be. A brief affair was not for her. There had been too many temporary relationships in her life. She wasn't going to walk willingly into another one, even with her eyes wide open.

She wasn't foolish enough to expect any permanent ties with John. She wasn't even sure she would want them. Her experience had shown her few marriages that worked any better than part-time involvements. She had seen the pain after relationships had ended, and the effects of divorce on families, including her own. Amy was a prime example of the disruption of lives, the instability and insecurity inflicted on innocent victims.

She wasn't going to allow herself to become involved with John. If that made her a coward, then that's what she was. A lonely coward. All she had to do was resist the magnetic pull of the physical attraction building between them. That was all.

An inelegant sound escaped her. That was all.

What a laugh. Keeping her distance, physically and emotionally, was going to be the hardest thing she had ever done in her life.

As the next two hours turned out, it was easier than she had expected. Amy took a glass of iced tea out to her father, walking slowly and carefully so she wouldn't spill a drop. While he drank it, he sat on the porch steps with her. Lauren purposely stayed in the cottage, leaving them alone.

When she saw John hold out his hand to show his daughter his dirty palm, it dawned on her why he had decided to do the yard work. He was demonstrating to Amy that he didn't mind getting dirty. He was more perceptive and sensitive than she had given him credit for.

John and Amy remained on the steps for a long time. Lauren had no idea what they were saying, but they were talking, or at least John was, and Amy was listening. Once when Lauren looked to see if they were still there, she saw Amy following her father around the yard, gathering sticks to put on the pile of debris he had made of other debris.

It looked like the weekend had been successful after all.

Both John and Amy needed to wash after working in the yard. John opted for a shower, then Amy splashed in the bathtub until Lauren called her to the table for lunch. Lauren had boiled the shrimp Silas had provided and sliced one of the sweet-potato pies for dessert.

After being shown how to peel the shrimp, Amy ...g in like a pro. She dunked each shrimp into ...tail sauce while regaling Lauren with how she ...ped her daddy clean the yard.

Lauren smiled at the little girl's excited chatter, sorry in a way that the weekend was almost over. But it was time to get back to Norfolk. As she began to clear the table, she told John they should be leaving soon.

He glanced at his watch. "Lauren, it's only two o'clock. What's the rush?"

Standing at the sink with her back to him, she squirted enough detergent into the pan to wash every dish in the cupboard. "I have things I need to do in my apartment."

John got up and walked over to Amy's chair. Bending down, he spoke softly to her, and the little girl hopped down from her chair and went into the living room.

John picked up their plates and brought them over to the sink. "Amy's in the other room, so you can tell me why you really want to leave."

Six

Lauren countered with a question. "What did you say to Amy to make her leave the room?"

"I asked her to dust the furniture in the living room. Don't change the subject."

"John, she helped me dust yesterday morning. How dusty can the furniture get in one day?"

"I watched her yesterday. She likes to dust. Answer my question."

"I forget what it was."

Exasperation made him throw his hands up. He paced several steps away, then whirled around to face her. "Why do you want to leave for Norfolk now?"

Stalling for time, Lauren plopped the plates and glasses into the hot water with more energy than was necessary. Soapsuds were filling the sink at a rapid pace. She made a sound of dismay as frothy bubbles splashed all over the front of her shirt.

Laughing self-consciously, she muttered, "For one thing, I need dry clothes."

"Lauren," he said with more than a hint of impatience. "I'm serious. Why do you want to leave before we have to?"

He wasn't going to let her off the hook, she thought. She grabbed a towel and moved a few feet away from him, needing the distance between them. As she dabbed at her shirt front, she attempted to keep her reply casual. "What difference does it make if we leave in an hour or at midnight tonight?"

"I believe that's what I just asked you," he drawled.

Irritation at him, herself, and the situation made her snap, "The purpose of this weekend was for you and Amy to get to know each other better. That's been accomplished. She is more comfortable with you, she speaks to you, she takes your hand, she told you when she needed to go to the bathroom, she showed you seashells by the seashore."

She clamped her mouth shut after her last statement, realizing she was beginning to sound batty. She knew her reasoning was weak, but she couldn't very well tell him she was becoming more and more obsessed by her feelings for him. The sooner she put the weekend behind her, the better it would be for her emotional sanity.

"That still doesn't explain why you want to leave early," he said. His gaze never left her face.

She knew he had a reputation for being relentless and tough in business dealings. Obviously in his personal life as well. Returning to her original reasons, since she couldn't come up with any others, she replied, "I have a few chores I need to do in Norfolk and so do you."

He leaned his hip against the counter. "I do?" he asked mildly. "What do I have to do in Norfolk I can't do here? You said yourself, the main purpose of this weekend was for me to spend some time with my daughter. That's what I've been doing."

"Mrs. Hamish is gone. You need to find another babysitter, remember?"

"I was going to ask your advice later this afternoon about getting a sitter for Amy, but since I'm running out of time, I'd better ask you now."

She didn't care for his sarcastic tone. Feeling defensive, she walked over to the table to finish clearing off their dishes. "I think you should look into a playschool for her during the day. You could drop her off on your way to work and pick her up on your way home. She would be with other children her own age during the day, which would be good for her."

John appeared to be frozen in place. He stared at her long and hard, finally nodding slowly. "As usual, you've come up with the perfect answer." He suddenly moved toward her as she was setting the dishes onto the counter. Taking her hands, he turned her to face him. "Except to the question I asked earlier. I want the truth. Why do you want the weekend to end before it has to?"

Striving for a nonchalance she was far from feeling, she said, "We'll stay then, if you're going to make such a big thing out of it. I just thought we would have an early start back to Norfolk. I was being ridiculously practical. I have things to do and so do you. I foolishly thought it would be easier to do them this afternoon rather than in the morning." She tore her hands out of his and made a dismissive gesture with one of them. "Forget I mentioned it. Wipe it out of your mind. I—"

He stopped her tirade by covering her mouth with his, effectively silencing her. He leaned back against the counter, pulling her into the cradle of his thighs. Frustration ate at him, mixed with the need tightening his arms and his body. Realizing anger was also riding him, he eased the pressure on her mouth. The current of desire between them changed as he kissed her more gently, his tongue seeking the warm recesses of her moist mouth.

Lauren rode the roller coaster of sensations as he led her from the hard passionate plateau down to the softer valley of sensual compulsion. Shattering pleasure took her over the edge and her body trembled against his. Lifting her hands, she slid her palms slowly around his waist, enjoying the feel of the corded muscles beneath the thin material of his shirt.

She felt caged by his arms and his body, yet she experienced a freedom from all inhibitions. The restraints she had put on herself had been severed, and she gave herself up to the delight of being in his arms. Leaning into him, she wanted to get closer to his warmth, his strength.

He lifted his head slowly, and his chest rose and fell deeply as he took a steadying breath. His dark eyes reflected the pulsing need surging through him as he looked down at her.

"It isn't this," he said, his voice low and husky.

With difficulty, she focused her eyes on his. "What?"

"This isn't the reason you want to leave. I thought maybe you were eager to get away from me." His hands stroked down her back to her hips, bringing her firmly against his lower body. "But you want me. I can feel it in you, just like you can feel it in me."

She arched her back, separating their upper bodies, yet pressing her hips against his. Previously she had not considered herself a sensual person. With John she became sensitized, all fire and heat. The coating of ice she wrapped around herself for protection melted when she was with him.

Slowly, reluctantly, she withdrew her hands from his back, placing them at his waist as she stared up at him.

After a long moment she couldn't hold his gaze any longer and rested her forehead against his chest. Her voice was muffled but audible. "Wanting doesn't always mean having."

"In this case it can."

She shook her head. Closing her eyes, she inhaled his masculine fragrance and reveled in the hard feel of him against her. Then she abruptly pushed herself away. Wrapping her arms around her waist to ward off the chill she felt at the sudden absence of his warmth, she murmured, "We agreed this weekend was for Amy's sake, John. Why complicate things? Tomorrow you will be Mr. Zachary and I'll be Mac. Everything will be back to normal."

He remained where he was, although he wanted her back where she belonged. In his arms. "The bracelet stayed where you put it, Lauren. I won't."

Her mouth parted in surprise. "What are you talking about?"

"You left the bracelet behind because you were becoming too attached to it. Now you want to put me and what's happening between us behind you, too, because I'm becoming important to you." His dark gaze held hers. "It won't work. I won't let it work. What we just shared can't be hidden away in a drawer because you're afraid you might lose it."

His perception cut her clean to the bone. Unwilling to admit he was right, she started to leave the kitchen. "You don't know what you're talking about."

This time he came after her. His fingers coiled around her arm, halting her and whirling her around. Framing her face with his hands, he said quietly, "I'm involved in this, too. Whether we stop now or go on is a decision both of us make, not just you. I don't know what it is between us, but I'm not willing to calmly shove it aside and forget about it."

The heat from his hands warmed her, yet she shivered. "I'm feeling anything but calm," she said huskily. "And I doubt if I could forget, but . . ."

He shook his head."No buts. All I'm asking is that you give us a chance to get to know each other better."

The ghost of a brittle laugh escaped her. "That's all? You don't ask for much, do you?"

His fingers combed through her hair, holding her still as he lowered his head. "I want it all."

So did she. Heaven help her, she thought frantically, as she felt his tongue slide over hers. She wanted it all too.

Rising up on her toes, she met him with equal force, her arms coiling around his neck. If there were going to be regrets later, at least she would have some memories to counteract them.

As he became immersed in her once again, it took every ounce of control for him to remember that his daughter was in the living room. He consoled himself with the fact that there would be other days, other opportunities to be with Lauren.

When he heard Amy's faint voice in the living room, he reluctantly withdrew from Lauren. "Fatherhood calls."

He had taken several steps away from her when she spoke his name. "John, I still would like to leave in an hour. I really do have things I need to do." Smiling, she added, "And to think about."

He didn't answer right away. The ticking of the old school clock in the dining alcove sounded loud in the silence as he studied her. Nothing had been settled between them, but his instincts told him this wasn't the time to press her.

Finally he nodded. "All right."

Lauren was surprised when he agreed. Her gaze followed him as he left the room. Raising her hand to tuck a strand of hair behind her ear, she closed her eyes. His scent was on her hands, on her flesh, in her soul.

It was too late. It was no longer possible for her to brush her feelings aside. What she had called infatuation a few days ago had somehow become much more serious.

She opened her eyes and wandered over to the sink, where she stared sightlessly out the window. This was one time her protective shell hadn't shielded her from caring. Making a derisive sound, she corrected herself. Who was she trying to kid? She was in love with John Zachary.

She had thought she was so smart, so clever in the past. It had been better to stay uninvolved, to protect herself from needing anyone. She had learned that when she cared for someone it hurt too much to say good-bye, when either she left or they did. Being tossed from parent to parent had left an indelible impression on her. She had adapted to different houses, new stepfathers and stepmothers, stepbrothers, stepsisters, half brothers and half sisters, even step grandparents, as well as to strange cities and temporary homes.

Until three days ago she didn't think there was any situation or any person she couldn't adjust to or live without. Which just went to prove she wasn't as smart as she thought she was.

Lauren had to hunt up a bag for Amy's new clothes,

as well as a box for the various shells and pieces of driftwood the little girl had brought back from the beach. The clay Lauren had given her had to go, too, so another container was found for that. And of course the pottery mug that Lauren had painted Amy's name on. John's car took a little longer to pack under the circumstances.

John went around with her to make sure all the windows and doors were locked and secure before they left a little after three.

The drive back to Norfolk was uneventful. Traffic, with people returning from a weekend on the Outer Banks, was usually heavy, and this Sunday was no exception. John was patient behind the wheel, unlike a lot of drivers who honked or zipped between and around other cars. Lauren taught Amy several silly songs, which helped pass the time until they reached the Norfolk city limits.

At a stoplight, John looked over at Lauren. "Do you want to go directly home, or will you have dinner with us?"

"I'd like to go home."

The red light changed to green. John brought his attention back to the street. "I couldn't tempt you with a juicy steak and a huge salad?"

"No you couldn't."

He was silent for several blocks. "There isn't anything I can say to change your mind?"

She glanced back to see that Amy was occupied with looking out the window. "You don't need me any more, John. You'll manage just fine with Amy." After a brief pause she said gently, "You have to be alone with her sometime, you know. It might as well be tonight."

John was silent for the length of time it took to go from one stoplight to another. Flicking a glance at her, he said, "You make it sound as though I'm afraid of her."

Lauren didn't say anything. It was what she thought, and she couldn't really blame him for feeling that way. Having the responsibility for a small child was scary, especially when John had no experience with children.

Lauren's silence was as loud and clear as though she had spoken, and John absently tapped the wheel. Maybe she was right. He was wary of being on his own with his daughter. He might as well admit it to himself. Lauren was also right that he had to be alone with Amy sometime. Where she was wrong was that he did not need her. He did, and not for the reason she thought. He wanted her for his sake, not just for his daughter's.

When he parked in front of her apartment building, Lauren carefully said her good-byes to Amy. The little girl looked from her father to Lauren, a frown appearing where a smile had been. She sat forward in her seat and placed her small hands on the back of Lauren's. "Why can't you come with us?"

"Because this is where I live."

"I want you to come home with me."

Lauren shook her head. "I can't do that, Amy." Before Amy could come up with another argument for her going with them, she added, "I'll tell you what. If it's all right with your daddy, you can call me on the phone after you've had your bath and are ready for bed. I'll give your daddy my phone number, and he can dial it for you."

Mollified somewhat, Amy nodded. "Okay."

Turning to John, Lauren told him her phone number. Reaching for her purse, she said, "Maybe I'd better write it down."

His hand came across the front seat and clasped hers. "I'll remember it."

John and Lauren got out of the car. He opened the back door for Amy and put her in the front seat where Lauren had sat. He fastened the little girl's seat belt securely, then lightly tapped her nose with his finger. "Thank Lauren for putting up with us over the weekend, Amy."

Amy obeyed, getting the phrasing a bit muddled. "Thank you for putting us up."

Laughing, Lauren replied, "You're welcome, Amy."

John lifted her bag out of the trunk, and she took it from him. "Don't bother walking me to my door. Amy shouldn't be left by herself."

Standing close to her, he ran a finger along her jawline. "I'm not sure you should be either. It's hard telling what you'll come up with in the way of excuses."

"Excuses? About what?"

"Why you shouldn't see me again."

Her smile was slightly off-center. "I'll be at work tomorrow. If I see you in the hall, I promise not to run for cover."

His fingers went under her chin as he leaned down. Against her mouth, he murmured, "Good. Then I won't have to come looking for you."

The kiss was brief but absorbing. His other hand rested lightly at her waist in an oddly intimate gesture. When he raised his head, his dark eyes held hers for a moment. Then she was left staring after him as he left her and got into his car. She lifted her hand automatically as Amy waved to her as they drove away.

Tightening her grip on her bag, she walked toward the entrance of her apartment building. She was experiencing a letdown feeling, an uncomfortable weight in the region of her heart. Yet she knew she had no one to blame but herself for feeling lonely.

As she entered the building, she tried to tell herself she had done the right thing in turning down John's invitation to dinner. She needed some time alone to think, to put the weekend into perspective. The problem was, she hadn't the faintest idea where she should start.

She was about to unlock her apartment when the door across the hall opened. Holly Steinmetz called out to her. "I have a package and some mail for you that came on Saturday."

"I'll be over to get them as soon as I put my bag inside."

"I'll bring them to you." Holly ducked briefly back into her apartment, then came out with a flat package and several envelopes on top of it.

By that time Lauren had unlocked her door and gone inside, leaving it ajar for her neighbor. Holly swept in and plunked the mail onto Lauren's coffee table before settling herself, her skirt swirling and bracelets jangling, on the couch.

Lauren's neighbor always dressed flamboyantly. Today she had chosen a full red skirt and an orange off-the-shoulder blouse, and a turquoise sash with fringe on the ends. Her hair was a mass of black curls held in some semblance of control with a rolled scarf around her forehead. Holly was twelve years older, four inches shorter, and twenty pounds heavier than Lauren. Single at the moment, she was the manager of a small bistro near the Raytech Building. She was open and frank, bordering on blunt.

Like now. Her expression was openly curious as she said, "I want all the dirt. Every juicy detail."

Lauren sank down wearily in the rocking chair several feet away from the couch. She really wasn't in the mood for an inquisition, but experience had shown her that trying to sway Holly in any direction other than the one she wanted to go in was a waste of time.

"Every juicy detail about what?"

"About your weekend with that sexy man who dropped you off out front. I just happened to be looking out the window when you got out of his car. I swear my windows steamed up when he kissed you." Her bracelets clattered as she leaned forward and rested her forearms on her knees. "Tell all. Don't leave out a single thing."

Knowing that Holly could be as persistent as an insurance salesman with quotas to make, Lauren gave her a condensed version of the weekend, with emphasis on Amy rather than on John. "So you see," she concluded, "it was sort of an emergency situation because John's babysitter had to leave suddenly."

Disappointment etched a frown on Holly's expressive face. Lauren hid a smile. If there was one thing Holly Steinmetz loved, it was romance. Which was one of the reasons she had four ex-husbands. The older woman loved being in love. It was being married she didn't particularly like.

Hoping to change the subject, Lauren glanced at the package Holly had placed on the table. "This is probably from my mother."

"That's what I figured. I noticed it had a Hawaii postmark."

Lauren removed the brown paper, then the birthday paper, and held the box out to Holly. "My hips are going to love this. Five pounds of chocolate-covered macadamia nuts."

Holly took several pieces of the Hawaiian candy. "For the sake of your hips, I'll help you eat them.

Now stop stalling and tell me more about the hunk you went away with for the weekend. I can't believe you could spend a whole weekend with this guy without the tiniest bit of hanky-panky going on."

"Sorry. There was no hanky and no panky. He came to the cottage with me because he wanted my help with his daughter. That's it."

Holly bit into a piece of candy. "And I suppose the kiss he laid on you was just gratitude. I stopped believing in fairy tales thirty years ago, cookie. You'll have to do better than that."

Lauren stretched her legs out in front of her on the braided rug. Sighing heavily, she admitted, "I think I'm making a giant fool of myself concerning John Zachary."

"It's real easy to do with men," Holly said lightly. "In what way are you making a fool of yourself?"

"Wanting more than I can have."

Holly reached for another piece of candy. "Why can't you have him? From what I could see from my window, he wasn't putting up much of a fight."

"There's a big difference between kissing a woman and caring about her. I'm not looking for an affair, Holly. I've never cared for being second or third in anyone's life. I've been there, and I don't want to be there again."

Holly was one of the few people who knew about Lauren's childhood. Living in proximity to her for over a year and being naturally snoopy, Holly had ferreted out various facts about Lauren's past. She was also aware of the lack of men in the younger woman's life.

"Maybe if you give him a chance, he could show you he's interested in more than just an affair."

Lauren shook her head. Her smile held a trace of

sadness. "Maybe not even an affair. As far as I know, he hasn't become involved with anyone at Raytech. He might decide not to start now."

"And if he does?"

"I told you. I'm not interested in an affair."

Holly's bracelets set up a minor din as she reached for the candy box again. "I thought you said you weren't ever going to get married?"

Suddenly restless, Lauren got out of her chair and walked over to a large fern in front of the only window in her apartment. Pulling off several dead fronds, she answered Holly's question.

"I don't plan to get married."

Holly nearly lost her sash as she abruptly pushed herself up off the couch. "I have to get away from that candy. It's affecting my hearing. I could have sworn you said you didn't want an affair, and just now you said you don't want to get married. That doesn't leave much of a choice."

"I know." Lauren walked to her desk and tossed the dead fronds into a wastebasket. "Now you see the problem. I'm in love with him, but I don't want an affair or marriage. As you said, it doesn't leave any choice except one."

"And that is?"

"I walk away."

Holly didn't care for Lauren's last option. "Doesn't sound like much fun to me."

"Me either. But it makes sense."

"Sense has nothing to do with it, cookie." Holly started walking toward the door. After she'd opened it, she grinned back at Lauren. "If it did, I wouldn't have four ex-husbands. Let me know what happens."

Lauren didn't move for several minutes after the door had shut behind Holly. Holly might think it was amusing to have been married so many times, but Lauren didn't. The older woman was another example of why Lauren didn't want marriage. Wedlock too often ended up in deadlock. Lauren didn't want her life divided into sections, with ex-husbands and possibly children scattered around the country.

She set about doing the chores she had told John she wanted to do. A load of clothes was washed, furniture was dusted, a grocery list was made, and several dresses and suits were set aside to be taken to the cleaners. The mundane tasks unfortunately didn't require any thought, leaving Lauren's mind free to wander back to the weekend spent with John.

Several hours later she was in the shower when she heard the phone ringing. Quickly shutting off the water and grabbing a towel, she hurried to the phone. A little out of breath, she picked it up.

Amusement colored John's voice. "You sound as though you've been running a race."

"I was taking a shower."

There was a pause, then he said, "Don't tell me you're wearing only a towel."

She smiled. "All right, I won't."

"So you are?"

"You told me not to tell you."

"So I did." He sounded slightly abstracted. "Listen, Amy wants to say good night. Ah, do you want to go get something else on before I put her on the phone?"

"No, I'm fine. The floor is already wet, and it's warm in here. The towel is enough."

"That's your opinion," he murmured.

Amy must have been right next to him. The little girl started chatting away, telling Lauren she had had her supper and her bath. For a few more minutes, she continued to talk, until she ended by saying, "Daddy wants to talk to you now."

A few seconds later John spoke into the phone. "As you can tell, we're surviving."

"It doesn't sound like your first night on your own has turned out so bad."

His soft male chuckle came over the line, sending shivers of sensuality across her skin. "I still have one more parental duty to take care of before she goes to sleep. She's chosen a book about a cat and a hat for me to read to her before she goes to bed. This might be the highlight of the night."

Lauren laughed softly. "Your daughter is opening up a whole new world for you. You'll become an expert on Dr. Seuss in no time."

"Among other things." There was a short pause. "The munchkin is clutching the book in her arms and standing right in front of me. I'd better take the hint and read to her. I'll talk to you later."

Lauren accepted his last statement at face value. "All right. Good night." She was about to hang up when she heard him say her name. "Yes?"

"Would you do me one more favor?"

"If I can. What is it?"

"Would you go put something on besides the towel? My imagination is working overtime at the moment."

It was odd how the tone of the phone call changed suddenly. Lauren's fingers tightened on the receiver. "There's an afghan on the back of the couch. I could wrap myself in that if you'd like."

He apparently could hear the amusement in her voice. "An overcoat would be even better," he muttered under his breath. Then he continued, "I have to go. Amy's becoming impatient. I'll talk to you tomorrow."

The line went dead, and Lauren slowly lowered the phone. She had meant what she said to him. She was pleased he was managing alone with his daughter. It was what should happen—for his sake as well as for Amy's. They could both get along now without her.

It was wonderful, she thought sourly, trying to find the enthusiasm she should have. Hiking up the slipping towel to cover her breasts more adequately, she returned to the bathroom.

It was just great.

Seven

Lauren went to work an hour early the following morning to make up the time she owed the company. There was no time clock at Raytech and Simpson didn't usually arrive until nine, so he wouldn't know she was keeping her word. But she did, and that was the most important thing.

It was doubtful her extra effort would have changed her supervisor's opinion of her anyway. Nothing would.

The one thing that remained constant, that she could count on to be there every morning, was the stack of paper work on her desk. Ever since she had come to work at Raytech, her supervisor had piled work on her desk above and beyond a normal person's ability to complete unless he was a computer. She wasn't. After she had learned why Simpson bore down on her more heavily than on any of the other contract clerks, she knew there was nothing she could say to him to change his animosity. All she could do was wade through the load of work he assigned to her.

During lunch with several co-workers, Lauren learned that John hadn't come into the office that morning and wasn't expected in the rest of the day. The women came up with imaginative reasons for Mr. Zachary to be away from the office, and none of them had to do with business. Lauren could have added fodder to the office gossip mill by telling them their employer was undoubtedly scouting out children's playschools. But she remained silent. For one thing, she didn't want anyone to know she was acquainted with John's personal life. Another reason was that the women were having such a good time coming up with their own ideas.

When she didn't hear from John the rest of the afternoon, she told herself it was for the best. Unfortunately she didn't believe that.

That evening she took work home with her. She didn't want to give Simpson the satisfaction of saying she couldn't do her job, and the work helped pass the empty evening hours.

Her phone rang at eight o'clock. In a rather hurried voice, John said abruptly, "Amy wants to say good night."

A few seconds later Amy began a disjointed account of her day. New toys were jumbled together with the description of a book bag her daddy had bought her because she was going to school.

Sounding animated and excited, Amy said, "Daddy said it will be great fun. 'Cept I have to have a 'fiscal' tomorrow before I can go to school. I want to go on a big yellow bus, but Daddy said I have to wait until I go to big school."

Puzzled about why John had sounded less than calm, Lauren asked, "What's Daddy doing now?"

"Shoveling bubbles."

Thinking she had heard wrong, she said blankly,

"I didn't quite catch what you said, Amy. What is Daddy doing?"

"Daddy bought me a bottle of bubble bath, and I poured it all in the bathtub. A lot of the suds fell on the floor. Daddy took my shovel and beach pail and is trying to put the suds back in the tub."

Lauren choked on a laugh. No wonder John had sounded harassed.

Amy apparently took shoveling bubbles in stride, going on to tell Lauren about her new "jammies" before she finished by saying, "Daddy said I could come and see you soon."

"We'll see, Amy. It sounds like you're going to be pretty busy for a while."

Amy wasn't about to be swayed. Her daddy had said she would be seeing Lauren, and the little girl stuck to it for a few minutes more before finally saying good night.

The next day followed basically the same pattern as the previous one. At least at the office. John was again absent. The paper work remained constant. At five o'clock, Lauren joined the mass exodus out of the building. Unable to stand the thought of going home to her empty apartment, she stopped at a posh French restaurant and blew a whole week's grocery allowance on one meal.

By the time she arrived home, it was past Amy's bedtime so she wasn't surprised or disappointed when she didn't receive a phone call. Or so she told herself. It wasn't past John's bedtime, unless he was keeping early hours since his daughter's arrival.

The following day as she went to the staff lounge to get a cup of coffee, she heard that the boss was back. Since he hadn't asked for her help the last couple of days, she figured he had everything under control. It was useless to tell herself she didn't mind that he didn't need her any more. She did mind. Not because he didn't need her assistance with his daughter, but because his kisses had led her to think he might just need her a little himself.

Around noon her phone rang. Not wanting to lose her place on the contract, she put her finger on a column of figures and answered it.

"Lauren McLean."

"I'll meet you in the lobby in five minutes."

"John?"

"Of course," he said, sounding amused. "Were you expecting someone else to invite you to lunch?"

"No, but—"

"I have a call on the other line. Lobby. Five minutes."

She was left listening to a dead line. As she replaced the phone she suddenly had a horrible thought. What if Amy was sick again? Guilt battled with concern. She shouldn't have allowed Amy to go wading in the ocean. She cursed herself for using poor judgment. She should have insisted on Amy's staying in the cottage even though the child would probably have been bored silly. Some expert on child care she turned out to be.

She set aside the contract and pushed back her chair. Standing, she glanced down at herself to check her appearance. Thankfully, her navy pinstripe shirtdress with its wide belt seemed almost as fresh as when she had put it on at six o'clock that morning. She grabbed her purse out of the bottom drawer of her desk, swept her brush through her hair, and left her office. Unfortunately, she ran smack-dab into her supervisor, who was coming down the hallway.

Simpson made an obvious gesture of looking at his watch. "Are we going out to lunch even though we have to work to do?"

Lauren was accustomed to his irritating habit of using the royal "we" every time he talked to her. It never failed to make her grit her teeth and bite back a sharp comment. She settled for using it herself. "Yes we are."

"Have we made up that time we needed to make up?"

"We came in early two mornings."

Simpson didn't seem to like that. Lauren knew he would have preferred to be able to find fault somehow, but at the moment he just couldn't come up with a way. Giving up, he stepped aside to let her pass.

She walked away from him, feeling the usual distaste from a run-in with her supervisor. It wasn't pleasant to be disliked, even by a supercilious jerk like Simpson.

She squeezed into the elevator with some of her co-workers who were taking their lunch hour. Being the last one in allowed her to be the first one out when the doors opened onto the lobby. She saw John almost as soon as she left the elevator. He was standing to one side of the building entrance, talking to a security guard.

The sight of him caused her heart to skip uncomfortably. He was dressed in a subdued gray plaid suit, white shirt, and red tie, his appearance elegantly professional—and compellingly attractive. As she approached he broke off his conversation with the guard and came toward her. He didn't appear to notice any of the people around her. His attention was focused solely on her, to the exclusion of everything and everyone else.

Smiling down at her, he said, "Right on time."

Lauren had to know. Unaware that her co-workers were watching with interest, she grabbed his arm. "What's wrong with Amy?"

He blinked. "Nothing. She's fine. I dropped her off this morning at a playschool recommended by a friend of mine who has two young children. I checked on her just before I phoned you. The woman I talked to said Amy was quiet and stayed to herself at first, but now she has made friends with one of the other children. The woman said Amy and her new friend were listening to one of the assistants read a story when I called."

Relief washed over her in waves. Suddenly aware of how tightly she was holding his arm, she loosened her grip and let her hand fall to her side.

John's eyes narrowed as he examined her face closely, noting her pale cheeks. "You were really worried about her, weren't you?"

"Children can get sick so quickly."

He took her arm and drew her toward the door. "She was checked thoroughly yesterday. She's in perfect health."

Walking quickly to keep up with his long stride once they were outside, she asked, "If Amy is all right, why did you make it sound so urgent I meet you?"

"I haven't seen you in two and a half long days."

When she looked up at him, he met her gaze, amused when he saw the surprise in her eyes. "You know, if you keep questioning the obvious, I'm going to wonder if your qualifications as an intelligent woman are overrated."

It was obvious, she wondered. To whom? Changing the subject, she asked, "Where are we going?"

"To get some lunch. There's a restaurant around the corner that has good food and no jukebox."

"Don't you like music?"

"Not blaring in my ear while I'm trying to eat."

The bistro where Holly was the manager was also

just around the corner, and Lauren had the sinking feeling that was where they were going. She was right. When they came to Holly's restaurant, John opened the door for Lauren. To her profound relief, Holly wasn't behind the cash register when they entered. She was saved from having Holly pounce on John with a thousand personal questions. At least for a little while. Holly was bound to see them when they left, but there wouldn't be as much time for her to talk to them then. She hoped.

When it looked like John was going to choose a table near the front of the restaurant, she suggested they sit in the back, away from the noisy bar area. The bistro did a rousing trade at lunch time, its main meal of the day. The service was quick and the food good, which drew people from the surrounding businesses regularly.

Walking ahead of John, Lauren chose a booth along one wall rather than one of the tables in the center. Each booth had a high back, making it a private alcove. She slid onto the cushioned seat, leaving the side facing the front for John. Except he wasn't going to sit across from her. She scooted over quickly when he sat down beside her. The booth suddenly seemed small and intimate as his thigh pressed warm and hard against hers.

A waitress came over almost immediately. She handed them menus, then left to give them time to decide what they wanted.

John ignored the menu and turned to Lauren. "I would like to read more into the fact that you prefer us to have some privacy, but it's probably only wishful thinking."

She faced him. "Why do you keep implying there's something between us?"

"Why do you keep insisting there isn't?"

Needing something to do with her hands, she fingered her spoon. "Because there isn't."

Sliding his hand from his own thigh to hers, he heard the spoon drop onto the table and felt her leg tense under his palm. "Isn't there?" he asked softly.

She was spared having to answer by the appearance of the waitress with order pad in hand. She attempted to remove John's hand from her thigh, but he simply turned his hand over and laced his fingers through hers.

He spoke casually to her, although the expression in his eyes was intimate. "What would you like?"

It took her a few seconds to realize he was referring to lunch. Without consulting the menu, she glanced up at the waitress. "I'd like a chef's salad and an iced tea, please."

John handed the menus to the waitress. "Make that two."

When the waitress had left the table, John turned sideways on the seat. He moved their clasped hands from her thigh to his. "Have you had a bad morning?"

"Not particularly. Why do you ask?"

"You're frowning."

"You're holding my hand."

"Is that why you're frowning?"

She shook her head. "You know you don't have to take me to lunch just because I helped you with Amy. You don't owe me anything."

"Good, because that's not why I wanted to see you." His thumb stroked her wrist. "What do you think about a puppy for Amy?"

The sudden shift of subject had her floundering for a few seconds. Smothering her disappointment with common sense, she asked, "Does she want one?"

"She asked me this morning if she could have a puppy. She said she asked Santa Claus to bring her one last Christmas, but he brought her a doll instead."

"What about you? Can you have a puppy in your apartment? A live animal isn't the same thing as a toy, and it's a whole lot messier. Even if you bought one that was already trained, you would still have to walk it several times a day." She hesitated before going on. "There's something else too. Something you should consider."

"What's that?"

"Unless you plan to keep Amy with you, it's not fair to her or to the puppy if you ship her back to her mother and the puppy has to stay here. Your ex-wife obviously didn't want her to have a dog, or she would have gotten her one last Christmas. Amy will become attached to the puppy and then have to leave it when she goes back to her mother. She's not going to understand why she can't keep the puppy. She'll be crushed."

He saw the shadows clouding her eyes. "Did that happen to you?"

"I was older than Amy," she said shortly.

John's thumb began to stroke her wrist again. He decided not to push Lauren to confide. "I've talked to my lawyer about getting custody of Amy. I'll put off the decision about a puppy until I know whether or not I'll have her permanently."

"Is that what Amy wants?"

"I don't know. She hasn't once said she wants her mother since she's been with me. Martine hasn't phoned to ask how she is or to talk to her. From what I can gather from Amy, she spent most of her time with a housekeeper. She doesn't seem to miss her mother. If I do get custody of her, I wouldn't be able to be with her during the day, but I'd be around at night and on the weekends. Apparently that's more than she had with Martine."

Lauren really wasn't surprised he had made that decision. She had seen for herself how much he cared for his daughter and wanted what was best for her. Still she felt compelled to warn him of the responsibility he was thinking of taking on.

"You've only had Amy for a short time. Are you sure you want her for the long run? She's already made a number of changes in your life. There are going to be a lot more."

He brought their clasped hands up to his mouth, his lips caressing her fingers briefly. "We can handle anything."

"We?" she repeated in disbelief. "As in you-and-me?"

He lowered their hands back down to his thigh. "You need it spelled out, don't you?"

"Yes, I think I do. I've never been very good at guessing games or mind reading."

"It's quite simple. I want to go on seeing you. Not only for Amy's sake, but for mine. I want to see you for lunch, for dinner, and after dinner." Something changed in his eyes. "Definitely for breakfast. And all the dark hours in between."

Lauren suddenly couldn't breathe. It should have been easy. It was something she'd done all her life, yet somehow his words had taken the air from her lungs. Was she really that surprised? she asked herself. She'd known of the attraction between them, the desire in his touch and in his eyes when he kissed her. She had recognized it because those same needs were deep inside her.

"I'm not interested in having an affair, John." Her voice was oddly shaken.

"Are you holding out for something more permanent?"

She detected a coolness in his tone, although there was no sign of withdrawal in his eyes. "There isn't any such thing."

"It's your turn to spell it out. Why aren't you interested in marriage?"

"I don't like divorce and what it does to people."

"We were discussing marriage, not divorce."

"One leads to the other."

He studied her for a long moment. He should have been relieved to hear her say she wasn't interested in marriage. It wasn't what he was offering. So why did he dislike her cynical tone of voice?

He found himself defending the institution of marriage. "Not all marriages end in divorce, Lauren. Some couples live together relatively happily all their lives. They raise kids, pay off their mortgage, and have their picture taken for the newspaper on their fiftieth anniversary."

"Maybe. All I've seen are the results of divorce courts, where children, houses, cars, and all worldly goods are argued over and then divided up. Two people who enter into a marriage with smiles and dreams leave the marriage with tears and angry words. I don't want any part of that, thank you. I won't be a part of tearing the foundations out from under a child."

"What about love? Don't you believe in that either?"

She looked away, unable to meet his intense gaze. "I believe there are different types of love."

He didn't much care for her answer. "You've told me what you don't want, but not what you do want. Do you know?"

She smiled wanly. "It's funny. I had almost this same conversation with my neighbor on Sunday. She didn't like my answer."

"Which was?"

It wasn't as easy to say it to John as it had been to Holly. She took a deep breath and forced it out. "I said I would walk away at the first sign of becoming involved with someone."

His expression gave nothing away, so Lauren was unable to tell how he was taking her statement. For a minute, he just looked at her. Then he slowly disentangled his fingers from hers. Without moving, he seemed to have distanced himself from her.

Lauren began to tremble, feeling as if she were about to shatter. She had expected to hurt when she made the break, but she had no idea the pain would be this severe. No matter how many times she told herself she was doing the right thing, a part of her still wanted to reach for that shiny apple at the top of the tree. The trouble was, she wasn't sure she would survive the fall this time.

The waitress approached their table and set their salads down in front of them. The glasses of iced tea followed, along with a basket of rolls and cruets of oil and vinegar. John shook his head when the waitress asked if there was anything else they needed. After she left them, he picked up his fork and began to eat.

Lauren didn't attempt to eat. It would have been impossible for her to swallow even a sesame seed. She only pushed the food around in her bowl, every nerve ending aware of the man who sat so close to her, yet who seemed so far away. John didn't make any attempt at casual conversation, obviously deep in thought as he ate his lunch.

When the waitress came back with iced tea refills, John asked her for the check. She provided it immediately. Sliding out of the booth after leaving a tip for the waitress, he extended his hand to Lauren. "We'd better get back to the office."

She took his hand and slid across the cushions. This would be the last time he touched her, she thought. Wrenching pain coiled through her stomach and tightened in her chest. It was over. Before it ever began, it was over.

The moment she was standing beside him, she heard a familiar voice saying her name. Turning her head, she saw Holly behind the cashier's counter. Her neighbor was attired more somberly for work than she normally was at home. Wearing a plain blue sheath, she had arranged a bright paisley scarf around her neck. Her usual assortment of bracelets was present, of course.

Lauren's shoulders slumped wearily. Salt was about to be rubbed in her wounds. Once Holly saw John with her, the older woman would undoubtedly have a field day.

There wasn't a hope in hell of getting past Holly without her seeing John. As she neared the counter, Lauren said, "Hello, Holly."

"Hi, cookie. I didn't know you were coming here for lunch today."

"It was a spur of the moment thing."

John had followed Lauren and was standing just behind her. Holly grinned. "Are you the spur of the moment thing?"

John looked at her blankly. "Pardon me?"

Rather than endure a game of twenty questions with Holly, Lauren supplied the introductions. "This is John Zachary, Holly. John, this is my neighbor, Holly Steinmetz."

If John noticed that Lauren hadn't qualified who he was, he didn't give any indication. He nodded in acknowledgment of the introduction. "How do you do, Ms. Steinmetz?"

Holly smiled broadly. "I'm doing just fine, Mr. Zachary. And please call me Holly." She accepted the cash and the check he handed her, punching the cash register automatically. Handing him his change, she tilted her head as she studied him thoroughly. "So you're the one causing my young friend here some sleepless nights."

Lauren groaned inwardly. Holly hadn't wasted any time.

John held his own with the outspoken woman. "That's only fair, Holly," he countered. "She's having the same effect on me."

Holly's laughter rang out. Turning her attention to Lauren, she said, "I see your problem."

Lauren smiled weakly.

Another couple had left their table and was waiting to pay their check. John put his arm around Lauren's shoulders. "We have something in common, Holly."

"We do?" the older woman asked, puzzled.

He drew Lauren toward the door. "I didn't like her answer either."

Holly's mouth dropped open. She stared after them as John gently guided Lauren outside.

When they entered the Raytech Building, Lauren was instantly aware of the interest she and John created in the other employees. Covert glances and open stares met them as she walked alongside him to the elevators.

One of John's assistants came up to him and immediately started talking about an administrative problem. While John was listening to his assistant, Lauren allowed herself to be swept into the crowd entering the elevator.

Back in her office she tried to concentrate on her work, but it grew increasingly difficult because she kept having interruptions. Some of the excuses for the visits to her office would have been laughable, if she had felt like laughing. Jane from the file room wanted to know where Lauren had gotten her dress. Theda from payroll was taking up a collection for her supervisor, who was in the hospital. There were three invitations to dinner, and one of her co-workers asked if she needed a ride home. Each person ended the conversation with a leading, semicasual reference to John Zachary, waiting with anticipation for her reaction. They were disappointed.

Using the excuse of being swamped with work, Lauren fielded their curiosity without giving them any additional fuel for the grapevine fire.

At five minutes to five, she tidied up her desk, then searched beneath it with her feet to find her shoes. Locating them, she kicked them out from under her desk and bent down to pick them up. She was slipping one on when the door to her office opened.

Expecting another subtle inquisition, she almost dropped her shoe when she saw who was standing in the doorway.

"Amy! Hi."

The little girl ran over to her. Hugging her, Lauren realized Amy was fairly crackling with excitement. It was a joy to see the child behaving normally.

"I went to school today, Lorn. I played with Kristen and ate peanut butter jelly sandwiches and built block houses and—"

"Why don't you wait until later to tell Lauren all about playschool, Amy?" John said.

Lauren looked up. John was leaning against the doorframe, his suit coat slung over his shoulder.

His gaze dropped to the shoe in her hand, then lifted back to her face. "Are you about ready to leave?" he asked easily.

Feeling foolish, she slipped on her remaining shoe. "Just about."

She opened her attaché case and placed a stack of papers inside. She was stopped from closing the lid by John's hand.

"What are you doing?"

"Getting ready to go home."

He picked up some of the papers and leafed through them. "With these? Why are you taking work home?" Without giving her a chance to answer, he opened the work log on the corner of her desk. His sharp gaze noted the number of entries, an astounding number for one person to get through.

He shut the log. "I'll have a talk with Simpson," he said tightly.

"I'd rather you didn't. It will only make matters worse."

"Lauren, he's overloading you with work." Tapping the log, he added, "You have enough here for three people to do. There are plenty of others to share the work load. It's ridiculous for Simpson to expect you to do all this yourself."

Amy tugged at her father's sleeve. "Daddy, you said we were going home."

"We're going, Amy. Lauren, we'll talk about this later."

"Daddy, I want to go home so I can show Lauren my new toys."

As though he'd never said a word about Simpson, he smiled down at Amy. "We're on our way." Then he turned the smile on Lauren. "We have our marching orders."

"Wait a minute. I'm not going with you. I'm going home."

"But, Lorn," Amy began. "You and I are cooking dinner."

Lauren stared at Amy as though the little girl had just spoken in a foreign language. She jerked her head up to look at John. "What is she talking about?"

He could see the confusion mixed with desire in her eyes. She probably wasn't even aware of the way she gazed at him, her feelings exposed for him to see. A tug of arousal tightened his body. He had wanted her in the last couple of days, but not as strongly as this. She could keep on fighting the attraction between them as she had at lunch, but eventually her passionate nature would convince her to give in.

A corner of his mouth curved upward. "We were hoping you would come home with us and help prepare dinner."

Lauren didn't know whether to laugh or cry. She did neither. "I don't think that's a good idea, John."

He lifted his hand to frame one side of her face. "I know you don't," he said gently. His thumb caressed her cheek. "I'll just have to show you it's more important than anything else."

Amy slipped her hand into Lauren's. "Please, Lorn. I want to show you what I made in school."

Lauren couldn't withstand the double persuasion of Amy's plea and John's touch. Raising her gaze to lock with John's, she said, "Promise me you won't say anything to Simpson." She saw a muscle in his jaw tighten and laid her hand on his arm. "If I agree to see you away from the office, you have to agree to keep the office separate. Heaven knows there's enough curiosity about us already around here."

Dropping his hand, John watched her closely. There was something behind what she was saying, but this wasn't the time to find out what it was.

"I won't talk to Simpson." Silently he added, "yet." "Now can we go?"

Lauren didn't immediately follow John and Amy to his apartment. It wasn't the way John wanted it, but she had reminded him she needed her car in order to drive home after dinner. He couldn't very well leave his daughter alone while he took her back to her apartment.

First she went home to shower quickly and change her clothes, exchanging her dress for a pair of white linen slacks and a navy blue silk shirt. While she was applying mascara, she suddenly thought of the way John had held her hand under the table at lunch and the soft touch of his lips on her fingers. Her hand jerked, leaving a black mark on her eyelid. She wiped the mascara off with a tissue, feeling foolish. Damn, she cursed herself. Just thinking about the man made her hand shake.

What in the world would she be like after spending hours with him in his apartment? She could phone him and tell him she had changed her mind. All she had to do was punch out his number and tell him she wasn't coming. Or she could go.

And reach for that elusive apple one more time.

Eight

Half an hour later, she rang the doorbell to John's apartment. The door opened almost before the bell had stopped chiming.

John reached out and pulled her inside. He, too, had used the time to change his clothes. He was wearing a pair of jeans and a loden green plaid shirt, the sleeves rolled up several times.

"I was beginning to wonder if you were coming."

"I was having a few doubts myself."

John gazed at her seriously. He had known of her wariness, her fears, her need for the security she thought she would find only within herself. The knowledge that she had overcome all of them to come to him gave him a sense of triumph unlike anything he had ever experienced.

Lowering his head, he kissed her briefly. "I'm glad you changed your mind," he murmured.

Unable to resist feeling her mouth under his again, he pressed his lips to hers. It wasn't enough. Not nearly enough. In such a short time she had become vitally important to him in ways he never expected or even thought he wanted. Needing to feel her slender frame more fully, he let his hands bring her hips to his. He saw the way her eyes changed and darkened as she felt his aroused body against her.

Her scent floated around him, intensifying his already fierce response. His arms tightened, his hand stroking her. "My Lord, you feel good." His tongue stroked her bottom lip. "I thought I had remembered how you felt against me, how you tasted. I wasn't even close."

For a few moments, they spun into a world of painful pleasure as he deepened the assault on her mouth. Primitive needs surfaced and pounded through them.

John reluctantly raised his head. "As much as I care about my daughter, I wish she were anywhere but here right now."

Lauren heard the raw urgency in his voice and realized it echoed her own. "Where is she?"

He released her slowly, his gaze never leaving her face. Hope and exultation flowed through him when he saw the extent of her arousal.

Taking her hand, he drew her down the hall. "She's in the kitchen. I told her she could put the drawings she made in playschool on the refrigerator door. We'd better get in there before she tapes the door shut."

They got there just in time to untangle Amy from the tape she had somehow gotten wrapped around her fingers. Lauren admired the drawings, relieved that Amy explained what each colorful scribble was supposed to be. Several papers contained an assortment of letters and numbers in different colors.

Lauren smiled down at Amy. "You've learned a lot in only one day, Amy."

"The last couple of days have been educational for me too," John said.

Glimpsing the amusement in his eyes, she asked, "In what way?"

He grinned. "I've learned why grocery stores put the racks of candy near the check-out counter. It's to drive parents crazy. While I was emptying the shopping cart on one side, Amy was putting candy bars in on the other side. I discovered little girls may be short, but they can reach an amazing assortment of toys in a store. Also, three-year-olds can ask the dam—darndest questions. I thought I was relatively smart until she asked me why the elevator goes up and down but not sideways."

Lauren laughed. For having had only a crash course in fatherhood, he was learning fast.

Later Lauren remembered the evening in a series of vignettes.

"I can honestly say I've never had a dinner quite like I ate tonight," she told John as they washed dishes. "Corn on the cob, SpaghettiOs, corn chips, and chocolate pudding cups are an interesting combination."

John handed a dried plate to Amy, who was standing on a chair in front of the kitchen cupboard. "They're all Amy's favorite foods."

"The meal," Lauren said dryly, "was definitely colorful."

"John, do you think there are enough toys in this bathtub? I can hardly find Amy."

"She likes to have a few things to play with while she takes her bath."

Lauren held up a soggy stuffed tiger. "Maybe you should help her choose next time. Preferably things that float."

"Good idea."

"Was it your idea to buy her that wristwatch, or was it hers?"

"She didn't have one."

"John, she doesn't know how to tell time yet. She doesn't need an expensive watch at her age."

"Well, she'll be ready when she learns."

After Amy was finally tucked into bed, John sank down on the couch. He sprang up almost immediately, and turned to pick up the box of crayons he had sat on. He set the box down on the coffee table, next to a coloring book, three pieces of furniture from a dollhouse, and a Barbie doll.

Lauren had an armful of toys and stuffed animals herself. "Where do you want me to put these?"

"Anywhere," he muttered as he sat back down.

She looked around the room. Except for the obvious signs of a child's presence, the furnishings in John's apartment could have come straight out of the display window of an expensive furniture store. The carpet was light gray, as were the drapes pulled back from the wide glass doors that faced the ocean. The couch and occasional chairs were upholstered in a deep green woven with threads of turquoise and gray. The tables were glass and brass, the lamps oriental porcelain.

It wasn't exactly an apartment designed with a child in mind.

She piled the toys she had picked up off the floor

on an upholstered chair. "Next time you go to the toy store, perhaps you should get a toy box. A big toy box. Maybe two."

When she was about to gather up more toys, he ordered, "Leave those. Sit down and keep me company. I'd offer you something to drink, but all I have is cranberry juice, something called juice in a box, and milk."

Curling her legs under her, she sat in a corner of the couch. "Having a little girl is causing a few changes in your habits, isn't it?"

"You could say that."

He rested his head on the back of the couch. "Tired?" she asked.

"Mmmmm. Up until Amy arrived, I thought I was in good physical condition. Training for the Olympics can't be as exhausting as keeping up with a tiny three-year-old."

"Maybe I'd better leave so you can go to sleep."

He flung out his arm as she started to get up. Grabbing her hand, he pulled her over onto his lap. "Stay. I've had to do without you for too long."

His thighs were solid and warm under hers, his arms strong and vital as he held her securely against his chest.

He sounded lazy and mildly curious as he said, "I tried to phone you around seven last night, but you weren't home."

"I had dinner at a restaurant after work."

"Alone?"

"Yes, alone. I splurged on an expensive meal instead of eating a TV dinner, which is all I had on hand at home."

"As long as you weren't working late." He raised his hand to halt any objection she might have made. "I know. You want to keep work separate, but we

can't completely ignore that you work for me, Lauren. I'm responsible for everything that goes on at Raytech. If Simpson isn't handling his department correctly, I have a right to know. If he's unfairly dispensing the work, I should know that too."

"If you go to Simpson with questions about the amount of work I'm doing, he's going to think I'm getting special treatment. You and I have been seen together several times, and the gossips are having a field day."

He watched her closely. "Does it bother you that people are talking about us?"

"It doesn't make any difference if I dislike it or not. The rumor mill will churn us around for a few days until there is something else to chew on." Getting back to her supervisor, she said, "I would prefer to handle Simpson on my own. I've never cared for people who used influence to get ahead. I certainly don't want to be thought of as someone who sleeps with the boss in order to keep her job."

"But we aren't sleeping together," he said quietly. "Not yet."

She smiled ruefully. "I doubt if others will be that broad-minded. As far as the grapevine knows, you haven't associated with any of the other women at Raytech. The fact that I've been seen with you several times is enough to cause curiosity and rumors."

"I don't like the thought of your having to take any flak because of me. If Simpson is—"

"Let me do my job, John. It's what you pay me for."

He sighed heavily, the sound a mixture of impatience and frustration. "All right. But if I see or hear he's treating you differently than anyone else in his division, I'll step in."

It was as much a compromise as she could expect.

She felt his chest move under her hand as he breathed deeply.

His eyes closed as he again rested his head against the back of the couch. "Maybe I'd better get some vitamins."

"Rough couple of days, huh?"

"It shouldn't have been," he said, sounding disgusted with himself. "Nothing I did was all that difficult. On Monday I took Amy to the grocery store with me, and we were in there for over two hours. It took twelve trips to carry everything up to my apartment. Another hour to put it all away. Then we visited eleven day-care centers until a friend of mine told me about the one Amy went to today. Yesterday there was the trip to the pediatrician which was quite illuminating. The difference between boys and girls was vividly pointed out to me when a nurse handed me a plastic container and said she needed a specimen from Amy."

Lauren's lips compressed as she held back a smile. "You have been busy."

"You don't know the half of it. Some of the toys Amy picked out at the toy store had to be put together, which by the way, requires at least a master's degree in engineering."

She valiantly swallowed her laughter. "John, you have a master's degree in engineering."

"Electrical engineering, not toy engineering. Believe me, my degree didn't do me any good when I had to put together a dollhouse where tab A did not go into slot B as it was supposed to. The instructions for the pump to the aquarium were in Japanese. Hell, it took over an hour to put the case of batteries I'd bought into everything that needed them. It's a mystery to me how one little thirty-pound girl can require so much stuff."

He was surprised to feel Lauren's body shaking in his arms. Her forehead was resting on his chest, effectively hiding her face. Placing his hand under her chin, he tipped her head back so he could see her. Her eyes glittered with amusement, and she was biting her bottom lip to keep from laughing out loud.

"What's so funny?"

His indignant tone set her off again. Her laughter flowed around him. When she could finally catch her breath, she apologized. "Sorry. All the times I've thought of you, I never once pictured you playing with toys."

He abruptly held her farther away from him. "You've thought about me?" Shock and disbelief were evident in his voice. "For how long?"

Lauren no longer felt like laughing. She could have lied or made light of her comment, but she didn't. "How long have I been at Raytech?" Answering her own question and his indirectly, she said, "A little over a year."

He stared at her. "That long? I never realized. I've always had the impression you didn't care for me much."

"It's annoying to be wrong, isn't it?"

His knuckles lightly stroked her cheek, leaving a trace of sensual pleasure in their wake. "This is one time I'm glad I am."

Needs accelerated as he took her mouth the way he had wanted to for what seemed like forever. Slanting his lips over hers, he sought the honeyed sweetness he knew was there. It was a taste he was finding necessary, unleashing a primitive hunger inside him to sample all of her.

The time for words was over. Sensations, hot and immediate, took over as his mouth and hands drew her down with him into the realm of passion. Tenderness mixed with demand. Hands enticed, flesh heated, currents hummed.

Lauren suddenly had the sensation of falling and savored the feel of his body covering her as she was pressed down onto the couch. She could feel his fingers tugging at her shirt, pulling it from her slacks. Her skin vibrated with the urgent stroke of his hand over her rib cage.

Her shirt fell away from her breasts, followed by her lacy bra. She gasped softly as he cupped her breast, his thumb tormenting and teasing her nipple into a hard, sensitized bud.

She unbuttoned his shirt. His chest was bare and hot under her hands. "John," she said breathily, needing to say his name, unaware of the aching demand in her voice.

"I know." His breath skimmed her skin as his lips closed over her throbbing breast.

Her eyes closed as she gave in to the riotous sensations heating her blood and searing her resistance. Instinctively her hips moved beneath his, seeking relief from the tension building inside her. Her legs coiled and writhed with his as she became embroiled in the sensual pull of the senses.

John murmured her name against her skin. Her ultimate response to him was everything he could ever hope for or want, nearly driving him over the edge. Craving became necessity. The level of his passion was close to the point of no return, and he held onto his control as fiercely as he held onto her.

When he felt her fingers at the waistband of his jeans, his stomach muscles clenched, and he shifted his hips away from her grasp. He needed the barrier of the material between them or he would be unable to resist taking her completely.

Breaking his mouth away from her breast, he buried his face in her neck. "No," he groaned roughly.

Lauren froze. Dazed, it took her a moment to realize what that single word meant. Shuddering against him, she whispered, "Why?"

Easing his long body up into a seated position, he took a deep breath, resting his forearms on his knees. "Amy."

Horrified, Lauren realized she had completely forgotten that his daughter was just down the hall asleep. John hadn't.

For a few long minutes they were silent as their blood slowly cooled. John turned his head to look at her and saw the tempting flesh partially exposed by her open shirt.

Feeling raw, he growled, "Fasten your shirt, Lauren. I'm barely hanging on as it is."

Her fingers trembled as she obeyed, her eyes stricken and wounded as her gaze met his.

Cursing himself under his breath, he sprang off the couch like a coiled spring. Stopping several feet away, he ran his hand over the back of his neck. "I can't believe I'm doing this."

He sounded as tortured as she felt. Lauren absorbed the feeling of rejection coursing through her, finding the pain more than she thought she could bear. She felt as though a priceless gift had been offered to her, then yanked away as she reached for it.

"You're right," she said quietly. "Amy might wake up and need you, or she could come looking for you. I—I understand."

"I'm glad you do. I don't," he said with an edge of frustration in his voice. He ran his hand through his hair. "I know you said you weren't interested in an affair or marriage, but you're going to have to make a choice between the two. We can't keep going on like this."

Stunned, Lauren stared at him. Swallowing with difficulty, she managed, "There's another choice."

"No! Walking away from me, from this, is not one of your options. If you were the only one involved, you could run away and hide from me, but I'm in this too. I know you're afraid of being hurt, Lauren. I'm not real wild about the potential of getting hurt either, but I'm not going to be a coward and pretend there's nothing between us."

She absorbed each word, feeling them flail her skin as though they were lashes from a whip.

John saw the uncertainty, the doubts in her eyes. Having placed his ultimatum on the table, he could only wait to see which choice she would make. He walked over to the sliding glass door and pulled it open. The strong wind coming off the ocean made his open shirt billow out as he stepped onto the balcony.

Lauren remained on the couch for a minute. She could see him leaning both hands on the railing of the balcony as he looked out toward the ocean. The wind tousled his hair roughly, yet he seemed to be bracing himself against more than that.

She was still reeling from his admission that she could hurt him. She had been so wrapped up in protecting herself, she had given no thought to his feelings. Guilt pressed down on her. Not only was she a coward as he had said, but she was also selfish. The admission came with difficulty, but once made, she accepted it.

She glanced down at her bare feet. She hadn't even been aware of slipping her shoes off. She put them on but didn't bother tucking her blouse back in. She looked around for her purse and finding it, gathered it up and hugged it to her.

Even with the wind blowing around him and the waves crashing onto the sandy beach, John heard the sound of his front door closing. He shut his eyes and hung his head. He couldn't even go after her. He couldn't leave Amy alone.

"Damn," he muttered under his breath. His very bones ached with wanting Lauren, and she'd gone. His fingers tightened on the rail. Somehow he had to find a way to be a parent and have a personal life too. Lauren was too important to lose.

Pain shot up his arm as the concrete rail cut into his fingers. Opening his eyes, he looked down at his hands and was startled to see another hand. Smaller, more delicate, and familiar, Lauren's hand lay next to his.

He jerked his head up. "I thought you'd gone."

The wind buffeted her hair around her face. "I did. I came back."

He reached for her, yanking her into his arms. His hold on her was possessive, his hands molding her to his hard frame. It was enough for now just to held her, to feel her alive and vital against him. Fierce joy and relief shook him, leaving him weak, yet stronger than he ever thought he could feel.

Her hands slid around his waist, and she rested her head on his bare chest. "I meant what I said, John. I do understand. Your daughter is important to you. That's the way it should be."

He loosened his hold enough to look down into her eyes. "You're important to me, too, Lauren." His hands cradled her face. "We need to figure out how we go on from here."

"Are we going anywhere, John?"

"Oh, yes," he said softly, his fingers threading through her windblown hair. "We're going a long way. It's just a matter of getting there."

Her mouth was taken with care, tenderness, and an underlying sensuality. The kiss lingered, gradually deepening as desire pulsed through their veins. The sound of thunder in the distance followed a flash of lightning over the ocean, adding a crackling intensity to the air surrounding them. The passion they created between them was as natural and as elemental as the storm building up in the heavens.

Several drops of rain fell, dotting the rail and their clothing. Breaking away from her mouth, John raised his head. The wind whipped her hair and she lifted her face to the sky as though challenging nature. Then she gazed at him, and her eyes shone with excitement.

Desire clawed deep inside him. She kept surprising him with the depths of feeling she could create within him.

"The ice is melting," he said huskily.

"What?" she asked, puzzled by his cryptic remark.

Unable to resist touching her, he gripped her shoulders. "You're a curious mixture of fire and ice. The fire is inside, covered by a shell of ice that keeps your passionate heat safe." His hands moved down to her alluring breasts. He smiled slowly as he saw the glaze of desire appear in her eyes. "The ice is melting," he said again.

It would be foolish even to attempt to disagree, since she felt as though her flesh were indeed dissolving under his touch.

After those few teasing drops of rain, the sky opened up in earnest, pelting them with a hard, steady downpour. John quickly drew her back inside his apartment and slid the door closed. Raindrops hit the glass, sounding like a machine gun.

He brushed a few drops of moisture off her cheek. "How about some coffee? We still have a few things to get settled between us."

A slash of blue-white lightning lit up the room, startling Lauren. A loud rumble of thunder followed. The rain continued with an unrelenting force against the glass door.

"I should go home before the storm gets any worse."

He glanced outside. "I don't want you driving home in this."

"Storms don't bother me."

Jumping when a bolt of lightning and a clap of thunder shook the glass door and reverberated through the room proved her a liar.

John shook his head. "I can see they don't bother you. Stay here tonight."

Lauren wasn't the only one disturbed by the storm. They both heard Amy's frightened cry. They went into her bedroom, and John scooped Amy up in his arms to comfort her. He leaned back against the headboard, talking to her in a low soothing voice. The little girl's arms wrapped around his neck, and she held on for dear life.

Lauren pulled the drapes across the window, shutting out the flares of lightning. There wasn't anything she could do about the thunder. The night-light John had turned on when he had put Amy to bed gave off enough light for her to walk to the bed without stumbling over anything. Standing there, she flinched when a particularly loud boom broke the silence in the room. She tried to hide her reaction, but she didn't fool John.

Patting the bed beside him, he said softly, "There's room for one more."

She didn't need any further persuasion. She joined them on Amy's bed, kicking off her shoes before settling herself snugly against John's side. "Just for a little bit," she said, "until it stops raining. Then I have to go home."

Smiling, he slipped his arm around her. "No problem. Just relax, and I'll tell you all about Busch Gardens."

"Why Busch Gardens?"

"I promised Amy we would go there one of these weekends." He described the various rides they would go on and the different sights they would see, his voice soft and low.

John could feel Amy's small body gradually slacken in his arms. Waiting a little while longer, he was about to put her down in her bed when he realized his daughter wasn't the only one asleep. Turning his head, he saw Lauren's eyes were closed, her breathing deep and steady.

With a crooked smile, he relaxed and stayed where he was.

Lauren woke suddenly when bright light shone in her eyes. She started to roll onto her side away from the sunlight but was unable to move. Opening her eyes, she saw that the sliver of light was coming through a slit of drapes covering a window. She stared.

The reason she couldn't roll over was that an arm was resting on her chest just under her breasts. Turning her head, she saw John stretched out next to her. He was lying on his side, his head sharing her pillow as he kept her securely against him with his arm. A quilt covered him from the waist down, leaving his bare chest exposed.

Lauren glanced at her own clothing. Her silk blouse was wrinkled but intact. She could feel the linen of her slacks against her legs. John had removed his own shirt but had left her fully clothed.

She lifted her hand to look at her watch. It was a few minutes after six. Easing the quilt back so she could get out of his bed, she started to roll over. His arm tightened around her.

"Where are you going?"

She turned her head and looked at him. "If I leave now," she whispered, "I'll have enough time for a shower before getting ready for work." Her fingers picked at the front of her shirt. "I don't think the boss would like me to be wearing these clothes when I show up at Raytech."

Propping himself up on an elbow, he looked down at her. "The boss would prefer it if you weren't wearing any clothes at all." He closed the space between them by leaning over to kiss her. "Good morning."

She licked her lips, savoring his taste. "Good morning."

His gaze locked on her tongue as it stroked her bottom lip. A groan of naked longing came from deep in his throat. "Someday you're going to do that to me."

"Do what?" she asked breathlessly.

"Stroke your hot pink tongue over my skin."

Need and hunger scraped across her like rough velvet, sensitizing her skin. Turning toward him, she buried her face in the hollow of his neck and shoulder, tasting his warm flesh with slow tantalizing caresses of her tongue.

"Like this?"

The combination of her moist tongue and warm breath against his skin had him moaning, his body shuddering with pleasure. "Yes," he muttered through clenched teeth. "Just like that. And more. Much more. Everywhere."

He pressed her onto her back, following her down as he took her mouth with blatant savage hunger. He unbuttoned her shirt and unfastened her bra so he could cover her bare breast with his seeking mouth.

Behind her closed eyes, Lauren saw colored lights exploding in brilliant flares as his mouth tugged and teased at her sensitive flesh. Her hand went to his hip to secure him against her, and she felt the rough material of his jeans.

Somewhere in a small recess of her mind that could still function, she remembered why John had stopped making love to her last night.

"John," she whispered. "Amy."

He lifted his head and stared down at her. What he saw in her eyes reflected his own desire. "I have to have you, Lauren. It would be like cutting off an arm if I stopped now."

"The door is open," she said weakly. But her hips arched into his aroused body, her movements contradicting her protest.

His weight was removed from her suddenly. He bent down and picked her up in his arms. His mouth ground against hers as he carried her into his bathroom, closing the door with his foot. He lowered her so she was sitting on the counter beside the sink, then reached over to turn the lock.

Her thighs clasped his hips, preventing him from moving away, although that was the last thing he was going to do. He removed her shirt and bra completely, and she lifted her arms to encircle his neck. Moans of gratification and pleasure were uttered, though neither knew who made the sounds as her breasts were crushed against his hard chest.

With deft, sure movements, John tugged off his jeans, then her slacks and slipped his fingers under the elastic of her panties. The marble counter was cool against her bare flesh, but she didn't mind the cold. Heat and fire flicked along her veins; love and desire swept over her in waves. Any doubts and fears she may have had about their relationship were overwhelmed. She loved him and she needed him. In her life and inside her.

"John, please. Don't stop," she begged, molten heat pouring over her and through her as he removed her panties and stroked her thighs. An aching pressure was building, and she felt as though she might explode. The world ceased to exist when his hands slid around her hips, and she felt his naked flesh pushing into her.

Her breath caught in her throat. Clutching his shoulders, she gasped for air, afraid she would shatter under the onslaught of ecstasy. Exquisite tension coiled as he surged into her again and again. As though from a long distance she heard him say her name, his voice oddly strained. Not able to speak, only feel, she answered with her body.

Passion's gate opened its tempting door, and they fell through together as the world exploded around them.

He didn't release her. He couldn't. John buried his face in her throat, breathing in her scent. One of them was shaking, but he couldn't tell which of them it was.

It cost him a great effort to raise his head. Brushing a damp tendril of blond hair from her cheek, he asked hoarsely, "Are you all right?"

She nodded, then changed her mind. "I'm not sure," she said faintly. "I've never felt like this."

He kissed her. "That's an understatement. Nothing has ever felt like this."

Gently separating from her, he stepped over to the shower and turned on the water. He returned to her and lifted her off the counter.

"What are you doing?"

He let her slide down his length. "You said you wanted to take a shower before you went to work."

Looping her arms around his neck, she smiled. "This isn't quite the way I planned to take it."

"Are you complaining?"

She shook her head. Water cascaded down on them, and she blinked the moisture out of her eyes. "Are we having an affair yet?"

His hands slid down over her bare hips. "Honey, we've been having an affair since that day I found you under the table in my office." He pulled her against him. "And it's going to go on for a very long time."

She didn't want to talk about tomorrow or forever. She drew his head down and raised up to meet his mouth. Now was all she could count on.

Nine

Lauren barely made it to work on time. Showering with John had taken a little longer than expected, but had been much more invigorating then her usual splash and dash.

After arriving back at her apartment, she kept staring off into space, remembering the last couple of hours, when she should have been changing into her work clothes. The shivers of reaction flowing over her were as vivid and as volatile as though his hands were actually stroking her skin.

She thought she had made it clear she wanted to keep their relationship separate from their work, but apparently John didn't take her seriously. He came to her office to take her to lunch and showed up again at five o'clock to escort her to her car. He made no effort to hide the fact they were together when they encountered any of the other personnel at Raytech. He openly held her hand as they walked through the lobby and put his arm around her waist in full view of everyone.

Objecting didn't do any good. John wasn't about to pretend. As far as he was concerned, their relationship was separate from the office. He didn't interfere with her work in any way except indirectly. Interoffice politics were alive in his company, as in most large organizations. Lauren's position could be adversely affected once it was known she was involved with the boss. If he saw or heard of any signs of prejudice or jealousy being directed at her, he would step in. Until then he planned to keep their respective positions at Raytech separate from their personal relationship.

That night Lauren again went to John's apartment. After dinner they played games with Amy, then tucked the little girl into bed. When she was asleep, they made popcorn and watched a movie on the VCR. Afterward Lauren said she had to go back to her own apartment. John tried to talk her into staying, but she refused. If he was serious about wanting custody of his daughter, she told him, it wouldn't help his case if his lover was living with them. Besides, Amy had enough to become accustomed to without having to adjust to a situation she couldn't possibly understand.

During lunch on Friday, when she mentioned going to the cottage for the weekend, he asked her to stay in town instead.

"John, you know I go to North Carolina every weekend."

"Is there any rule that says you can't drive down on Saturday?"

"Well, no, but . . ."

"Do you own a beautiful dress?"

She blinked. "Yes. Why?"

"I want you to put that dress on and be ready by

eight o'clock tonight. We're going out. Just the two of us."

"What about Amy?"

"Remember I mentioned my friend who told me about the playschool?"

She nodded.

"He has three children he loves dearly, but once in a while he and his wife like to get away from them. They have this terrific babysitter who loves children and doesn't eat them out of house and home or drink all their booze. She doesn't have a boyfriend who shows up the minute they leave the house and she doesn't use their phone to call Timbuktu. Amy has met her and seems to like her, so I asked the woman to come over at seven-thirty to watch Amy. You and I are going to venture out all by ourselves like regular people. It will give us a chance to talk without interruptions."

"Talk? What about?"

"Haven't you heard that patience is a virtue?" Glancing around Holly's crowded restaurant, he added, "This isn't the time or the place. I want you all to myself without the possibility of Holly or anyone from the office stopping by to chat."

After she returned to her office, Lauren pondered several possibilities of what John wanted to talk about, but couldn't come up with anything that made sense. Except that he wanted to have privacy to tell her their brief relationship had run its course and he was ending it. She didn't care for that particular thought, but it kept popping up no matter how she tried to push it away.

When she stepped out of the elevator at the end of the day, John was waiting for her. He took her arm and walked beside her to the parking garage. "Why are you late getting off work?"

"I had a few things to do."

He stopped, forcing her to halt too. "Is Simpson piling the work on you again?"

"John," she said warningly.

He started walking again. "I know. You want me to butt out. It's fairly difficult, considering I'm the one who's supposed to be in charge at Raytech," he said dryly.

When they reached her car, he opened the door for her. Cupping her chin in his hand, he held her still while he bent his head and kissed her. Lingering over her lips, he murmured, "I'll be at your apartment at eight."

Would he kiss her like that if he meant to say good-bye? she asked herself as she studied him after he raised his head. She didn't find the answer in his expression.

He gently pushed her behind the wheel of her car. "Drive carefully. The life you save is mine."

As she drove away, she wondered why she felt as though she had just been run over by a subtle steamroller. Her plans for taking one day at a time had been working just fine until now. Well, almost fine. John continually touched her and kissed her whenever they were alone for a few minutes. However they hadn't made love again. She told herself she should be happy just to be with him. And she was. But after knowing the pleasure of making love with him, she couldn't help regretting they hadn't been able to be together intimately.

At least for her the term making love had applied. She had been able to express her need for them to be as close as two people could possibly be. Still she couldn't help wondering how John defined their intimacy. Physical gratification wasn't the same as love. She shook her head in irritation at herself. Again she was being greedy, wanting everything rather than being content with what she had.

The driver behind her honked, and she realized she was barely creeping along the road. She'd better pay attention to her driving if she wanted to get home with all four fenders intact.

By the time she arrived at her apartment, she had almost two hours to prepare for the evening with John. If tonight was going to be her swan song, she was going to do her best to look like one, rather than like an ugly duckling.

From the back of her closet, she took out a garment bag. Unzipping it, she removed a black silk dress from a padded hanger. The material was delicately textured with soft threads that glittered in the light. It was fully lined, which eliminated the need for any underclothing except black lace bikini panties and the narrow strip of a garter belt and stockings. Thin spaghetti straps and a low-cut back exposed her slender shoulders and an expanse of her back.

The only jewelry she wore was a rhinestone comb that swept her hair back on one side. Plain black heels and a small evening purse completed her ensemble, and she was satisfied when she scrutinized her appearance in her full-length mirror.

Later when she opened the door to John, she was amused and pleased to see the stunned expression in his eyes. "You're looking at me as though you've never seen me before."

Leaning against the doorframe, he said huskily, "I haven't. Not like this. Do you need me to tell you how beautiful you are?"

"It would be nice to hear."

"I don't have the right words. I don't think there are appropriate words."

She smiled. "Thank you. That will do nicely."

She frankly admired him, too, dressed in a light tan sport coat, dark brown slacks, white shirt, and sable brown silk tie. "Would you like to come in?"

He shook his head. "If I come in, we won't be going anywhere for quite some time."

Lauren didn't look away from his intense gaze for a long moment. He had to know she wouldn't object if he chose to stay there instead of going out. But he smiled and held out his hand.

She took it and left with him.

She had taken it for granted they would be going to a restaurant, but she couldn't have been more wrong.

Her first indication of where they were going was when John drove to the waterfront in Norfolk. She walked beside him past several boats, her heels echoing on the wooden boards of the dock. He stopped at a gangway leading to a forty-foot motor yacht, which had a fly bridge complete with a man standing at the helm.

"Is this boat yours?" she asked in astonishment.

He took her hand and helped her aboard. "Only for the next three hours."

He slid open a glass door and gestured for her to enter the cabin. Lauren stepped inside, her heels sinking into thick, luxurious pale blue carpet. She saw a table set for two with spotless china and sparkling crystal on a linen tablecloth. Plush white chairs had been placed at the table, matching the couch along the starboard side. At each place setting was a silver dome covering the plate. An oriental screen separated the galley from the lounge.

John pulled out a chair for Lauren. He struck a match and lit the two candles, then pushed a button attached to the bulkhead. She didn't hear anything, but apparently the man on the fly bridge did. The engine started. Through the wide window next to the table, she could see two men untying the bow and stern lines. In a few minutes the waterfront began to recede as the boat moved away from the dock into the Elizabeth River.

John poured wine into the crystal goblets and held his glass aloft as though making a toast.

Slowly Lauren raised hers to clink with his. "You've gone to a lot of trouble. Dinner at any restaurant would have been sufficient."

"Not for tonight. Restaurants have waiters and other people. Here we have privacy. There is a crew of three, and they have instructions to take the boat out into the Chesapeake Bay for three hours. I figured that would give us plenty of time."

She took a sip of wine, then toyed with the stem of the glass. "At first, I thought this was an extravagant way for you to say good-bye," she said lightly, as though it really didn't matter. Then she smiled. "Now I'm beginning to wonder if you have seduction in mind."

His eyes narrowed. "Good-bye? Why would I be saying good-bye?"

"It happens. During the last couple of days, you have to admit you've shown signs of being more than slightly discontented with the way things were going."

"Lauren," he began, reining in his impatience. "What you saw was frustration, plain and simple. If the circumstances had been different, I would have kept you in bed the rest of the week." He saw the way her eyes changed, darkening with desire. "I thought wanting you was going to drive me crazy before we made love the morning after the storm. Afterward I wanted you even more. I still do. Having Amy with me is more inhibiting than I expected."

"I know," she murmured. Gesturing to include all of the boat, she asked, "Is that why you resorted to this? A few hours of privacy?"

"That's part of it."

"What's the rest of it?"

He was nervous. John realized that with a sense of shock, then accepted it. How odd, he thought, to be apprehensive after all the planning he had put into tonight. He realized it was because he didn't know what her answer would be. Suddenly, too restless to stay seated, he pushed his chair back and took several paces away from her.

For a long moment he simply stared out the opposite window. The next few minutes could be the most important in his life. He couldn't rid himself of the feeling he was balancing precariously between heaven and hell. Lauren's answer would determine which it would be.

Steeling his nerve, he slowly turned. "Lauren, I want you to marry me."

She dropped her wineglass and stared at him. Neither of them noticed or cared about the spreading stain on the once immaculate tablecloth.

Tension hung in the air as their gazes held. Breaking the silence finally, Lauren murmured, "John, you know how I feel about marriage. I've been honest with you from the very beginning."

He shouldn't have been disappointed at her answer, for it was what he had expected. "Yes, you have. You've been very specific about just what you do and don't want. You don't want marriage, you won't live with me, and you won't spend the night at my apartment. I have all your don'ts engraved in my brain. The problem is your options leave no options. Something has to give, Lauren. We can't go on the way we have the past few days."

"And you think marriage is going to solve everything?" She rose from her chair and walked over to the sliding glass door to look out at the Navy ships docked at the naval station. Feeling a sudden chill that had nothing to do with the temperature, she hugged her arms. "Marriage would only complicate things, John. Not make them simpler."

Closing the space between them, he took her arm and turned her around. "We would be able to be together. Not for just a few hours every evening playing a game with Amy and then my walking you to your car. I want to reach out at night and find you beside me. I already feel like my life is in segments. Amy in the morning, work during the day, you and Amy for a few hours in the evening, then I'm alone the rest of the night. Our marriage would tie everything together."

She had listened very carefully but hadn't heard him say anything about love. Not that it would make any difference. She loved him yet still didn't want to marry him.

She looked away from him. "All the times my mother has gotten married, she never once said it was for convenience."

He heard the dry bitterness in her voice. Suddenly it occurred to him what she meant. For all his planning, he had done this badly.

"Lauren," he said gently. "I want to marry you because I love you. I want to be with you because I love you. I want to sleep with you because I love you." Framing her face with his hands, he repeated simply, "I love you."

Lauren stared at him, seeing the truth of what he said in his eyes. She had been wrong. Love did make a difference. Her head fell forward, and she rested her forehead on his chest. "You're not making it easy for me to refuse."

"Good." He put his arms around her, his hands sliding over her bare back. He fought his disappointment in not having his declaration of love returned. "I don't want you to refuse. I want you to say yes."

Without being aware of it, she arched under the feel of his warm hand on her naked flesh. "I don't know."

Relief flowed through him in an overwhelming tide. At least she hadn't said no. Lowering his head, he took her mouth with a mixture of hunger and tenderness. Desire rushed to meet need as the kiss deepened.

Shivers of reaction spread through her. Needing to feel him closer to her, she pushed his coat off. Then her fingers went to work on the buttons of his shirt, but they were shaking too badly to accomplish the task.

John tore his mouth away to caress her throat with his lips. His hand closed over her trembling fingers. "I didn't bring you here for this."

"I know." Her hand slid through the opening she had made in his shirt, stroking his heated skin. "Make love to me, John. Make me believe you really love me."

The combination of her touch and her plea undermined his need to get their future settled tonight. Other needs became more urgent.

Lauren raised up on her toes and trailed her lips over his throat. Nipping gently, she felt an exhilarating joy at his response as he groaned and tightened his arms around her. She filled herself with his male scent, glorying in his nearness.

John scooped her up in his arms and carried her past the oriental screen and down the passageway into the stateroom. Still holding her, he kissed her passionately, his tongue intimating what was to come. Easing her down until she was standing in front of him, he unzipped her dress and slipped the narrow straps off her shoulders.

Keeping her gaze locked with his, Lauren stepped back and lowered her arms. Her dress slid down onto the floor. John's heart thudded heavily in his chest. Moonlight reflecting off the water shone through the portholes enough to illuminate her skin.

She reached up to loosen his tie. "I've never undressed a man before."

"I'll let you know if you do it wrong."

The tie was dropped onto the floor. His shirt followed. She raked her nails down his chest and heard his quick intake of breath.

He brushed her hands aside abruptly. "As much as I'm enjoying this, I believe I'll help you."

The rest of his clothes were removed swiftly, then he lifted her up and laid her on the large bed. His fingers slipped under the strip of narrow black lace, gliding over her hip and her thigh to eliminate that last barrier between them.

The impact of naked flesh against naked flesh was

a shattering pleasure as hands caressed and stroked and aroused. Mouths teased and tormented while legs entwined.

It was as though the boat had been sucked down into a whirlpool of sensation and the two passengers along with it. Waves of ecstasy crashed over them as John eased into her. She sighed his name, and he groaned as he felt the slight sting of her nails on his back.

Together they were pulled beneath the rippling surface of sanity into a wild tumultuous sea of sensual delight. Grasping the last remnants of his control, John drove her up but wouldn't let her go over the edge.

"Tell me what I want to hear," he ordered hoarsely.

Lauren arched her hips to force him to continue, but he was adamant.

He had to have it all. "Tell me."

She whimpered softly, unable to fight him any longer. "I love you."

John wasn't satisfied. He had to know she knew whom she was saying it to. Moving against her slowly, tormenting them both, he demanded, "Say my name."

Frustration flashed in her eyes, blending with the desire he had stoked to a fever pitch. "I love you, John." She made a demand of her own. "Love me." Sliding her hands under his, she threaded her fingers through his and gripped them hard. "Please. Now."

Shuddering at the sweet agony of being wanted, John thrust into her again. Tightening his grip on her hands, he drove her up and over the edge of ecstasy, accompanying her every inch of the way.

The storm subsided gradually. John hadn't left her, and still held her hands. Slowly he raised his head from the hollow of her throat. "I wasn't fair, was I?"

Luxuriating in the wonderful aftermath of his lovemaking, she said, "All's fair in love and war." She moved her hips slowly, seductively, smiling as she felt his response deep within her. 'This isn't war, is it?"

"No." He kissed her deeply. "This is love."

The incredible dance of love started all over again. This time he took her with less urgency and with a subtle sensuality that had her twisting and writhing under him. Together they reached for the sweet madness waiting for them, their voices crying out simultaneously as they crested and fell over the edge.

John reluctantly zipped up her dress. "It's a shame to have to cover all that beautiful skin, but I wouldn't want to shock our crew."

She bent down and picked up his tie, folding it over several times and stuffing it into the pocket of his coat. She was horrified to realize she hadn't given a thought to the three men on the boat with them. Hugging his coat, she said, "I'm not sure I like the idea of those men knowing what we've been doing."

He took his coat from her, then led her back into the lounge. "As far as they're concerned, I chartered the boat so I could have dinner in privacy with my fiancee."

She sat down at the table. "But we aren't engaged."

He removed the silverdome from her plate, then from his own. Sitting down across from her, he said casually, "Not officially."

She ignored the food in front of her. "You're very confident, aren't you?"

He reached over and took her hand. "I know this has happened too fast for you, Lauren. That doesn't mean it isn't right. I have to admit I didn't expect to fall in love so quickly myself. I know you have your doubts, and I can even understand why you have them. I'm asking you to trust me, to trust what we have going for us."

Her gaze was on his hand. After a long moment she turned hers over and clasped his. "I don't have a choice." She raised her eyes and met his intent look. "I'll still not sure marriage is the answer, John, but I am sure how I feel about you."

"That will do for now. I'll wait for the rest."

Ten

On Saturday morning they drove to the cottage in North Carolina. Amy helped Lauren remove the fine film of dust that had accumulated on the furniture during the past week, while John raked up beer cans and other debris from the porch. Apparently teenagers had taken advantage of the empty cottage and used its porch for a party. At least they hadn't broken into the house, which happened from time to time in some of the cottages in the area.

It was remarkable the changes a week had made in Amy, Lauren mused as the day passed. The little girl whisked a dustrag around while singing a nursery rhyme she had learned in playschool. She had to be told to pick up her toys and not to run in the house. During lunch she had to be instructed not to talk with her mouth full when she started to tell Lauren about a game she learned in playschool. She was more openly affectionate now, distributing hugs and kisses whenever she felt the occasion warranted them. She was acting like a normal healthy child.

Lauren noticed Amy was still careful not to get dirty, but she wasn't as fanatical as she had been. Proof of how far the little girl had come in such a short time was seen when Amy crawled around in the wet sand helping John build a sand castle. Sand clung to her bathing suit, her knees, and her hands as she scooped up handfuls of it and patted them into place.

It was while they were at the beach that John brought up the subject of Amy living with him permanently. He sat back on his heels and watched his daughter closely for her reaction.

A small frown appeared on the child's face. "What about Mommy?"

"We could fly out to California to visit her."

"All of us?"

John looked at Lauren. "Maybe." Then he brought his attention back to his daughter. Presenting his case as fairly as he could manage under the circumstances, he said, "I would like to have you live with me permanently, Amy. That would mean seeing your mother briefly, not all the time."

"Would Lorn live with us too?"

A corner of his mouth lifted in a half-smile. "That's up to Lauren."

Amy's little face was solemn as she thought over what her father had said. "Could I still go to play-school?"

He nodded.

"Do you think Mommy will be mad if I want to stay with you?"

If Martine became angry, John thought, Amy would never know about it. At least not from him. "I'll talk to Mommy."

Springing up, Amy threw herself at her father.

Sandy arms were flung around his neck as she said, "I want to stay with you."

John's arms came around the small, precious bundle, his gaze meeting Lauren's over Amy's head.

"One down, one to go," he said with quiet determination.

After they returned to Norfolk on Sunday evening, John told Lauren of his plans for the next day. Amy had accompanied them up to Lauren's apartment and was wandering around. John had joined Lauren in the kitchen, where she was making coffee.

"I have a big favor to ask of you," he said.

Silently counting scoops of coffee, she asked, "What kind of favor?"

"I'd like you to stay at my apartment with Amy while I'm gone."

Some of the coffee grounds spilled on the counter as she jerked her head around. "Gone? Where are you going?"

"The contract with the Status Brothers has to be signed, which means a trip to California. I put them off until Tuesday so I can go to San Francisco first to talk to Amy's mother. I can't very well leave Amy alone while I'm gone."

"Which is where I come in."

He took her hands and turned her to face him. "I need to get things settled with Martine, Lauren. Amy's custody isn't something I can discuss on the phone."

"Are you expecting her to object?"

He shrugged. "I won't know until I talk to her in person." With the casual intimacy of a lover, he combed his fingers through her hair. When his hand cupped the back of her head, he drew her toward him. He touched her mouth briefly with his, then raised his head. "The next several days with Amy will give you a chance to see if you want to take on a ready-made family when you marry me."

"John, you're pushing again."

He sighed. "I know," he said, resting his forehead on hers. If he had his way, he would be pushing harder. A slight smile curved his mouth. "You might as well get used to that too."

The following morning when he dropped Amy off at playschool before catching his plane, John made arrangements for Lauren to be allowed to pick Amy up. Hoping he had taken care of everything, he boarded the plane, determined to talk to his ex-wife about their daughter.

He called Lauren later in the evening than he had planned. Sounding weary to the bone, he asked how her day had gone.

Making herself more comfortable, she propped a pillow against the headboard of his bed. She held the receiver tightly, wishing he were there with her. "Amy was disappointed when she couldn't talk to you tonight, but I told her you would have called if you could have. Are you in San Francisco or Los Angeles?"

"Los Angeles. Martine wasn't home. Her neighbor said she'd left that morning carrying a suitcase. All I could do was contact her lawyer and tell him my lawyer would be getting in touch with him about a custody hearing."

Lauren knew a custody hearing would be necessary, but she didn't want to discuss it. Having been the object of such hearings herself, they were not her favorite topic of conversation.

"There are now two new paintings on the refrigerator," she said. 'We're either going to have to get a bigger refrigerator or find another place to display Amy's art work."

John's frustration eased a little when he heard her say "we" instead of "you." Whether she was aware of it or not, she was automatically including herself in the decisions to be made in his household. Some of the tension between his shoulders dissipated. Maybe things weren't as hopeless as they had seemed earlier that day.

He changed the subject abruptly. "Which phone are you using?"

"The one in your bedroom."

There was a brief silence on the line. "Are you in bed?"

"Mmmmm. I was about to turn off the light when you called."

"Do it," he said. There was a rough quality to his voice that had nothing to do with command and everything to do with sensuality.

At first Lauren didn't understand what he wanted. When she did, she held the phone toward the lamp as she clicked off the switch so he would hear it.

"The light is out," she said. "I'm lying on the side next to the phone."

"That's where I usually sleep," he murmured.

She smiled. "Do you want me to move over?"

"No. Stay where you are. It's where you would be if I were there."

She closed her eyes as waves of heat flashed through her. "I wish you were here now."

A groan came from deep inside him. "Hell, so do I. If I don't hang up, I'm going to be in worse shape then I already am. I like the thought of you in my bed. It's where you belong, but it's killing me that I can't be there with you." Sighing heavily, he added, "I love you, Lauren. Good night."

Moisture gathered in her eyes, and she shut them tightly. "Good night, John. I love you too."

After she had hung up the phone, Lauren rolled over and hugged the pillow next to hers, which was a poor substitute for the man she loved. If she refused to marry him, there would be many other lonely nights like this one. Marriage to him would present an uncertain future, but without him, she had no future at all.

In the morning, Lauren managed to get herself and Amy out the door in time to deliver the little girl to her playschool and herself to work without any difficulty. In fact she had enjoyed fixing Amy's breakfast, cajoling her into eating, and answering the child's numerous questions as she applied her makeup in John's bathroom. She had walked Amy into school, then bent down to kiss her, promising to be there in the evening to take her home. She had watched Amy skip into the classroom with an odd sense of pride, as though the child were her own.

When she returned to her office after lunch, there was a phone message to call the playschool immediately. With her heart in her throat, she punched the numbers for the school and waited impatiently for someone to answer.

After the third ring, a woman answered. Lauren told her who she was and that a message had been left for her to call.

"Is Amy all right?"

The woman's voice was unruffled and calm. "Amy is fine. The reason I phoned, Miss McLean, is because a woman came here this morning insisting she was Amy's mother. She wanted to take the child with her, but as you know, we don't release the children to anyone other than the people authorized by the parent. Our contract is with Mr. Zachary, who has only himself and you on record as being responsible for Amy Zachary."

A sliver of fear insinuated itself in her stomach. "Did the woman give her name?"

"She said she was Mrs. Zachary, but when I asked for identification, her driver's license had a different name, Martine Tremaine." The woman paused, then added, "The problem is this woman said she would be returning with the police, Miss McLean. She said she had a legal right to the child. It will be extremely upsetting to the other children if policemen descend on the playschool."

Without giving the woman a chance to say anything further, Lauren said, "I'll be right there."

She slammed down the phone, grabbed her purse, and rushed out of her office. She stabbed the elevator button impatiently several times and finally the doors slid open. Intent on getting to Amy, she didn't notice Simpson getting off the elevator until she bumped into him.

"Excuse me, Mr. Simpson," she murmured as she tried to step around him to enter the elevator.

"Where are we going, Miss McLean? I believe we've already had our lunch break, haven't we?"

She was in no mood for his sarcasm. "I have a personal emergency, Mr. Simpson. I must leave right away."

He was so taken aback by her statement, he neglected to use his normal condescending way of speaking. "You were just going to walk out without checking with me first?"

Several of the office staff had stopped a few feet away, blatantly curious about the confrontation in front of the elevator.

Lauren's priority was to get to Amy. If she had to go through or around her pompous supervisor, she would. "It's important that I leave immediately, Mr. Simpson. Please get out of my way."

Highly indignant that she was disregarding his authority, Simpson didn't budge. "You will come to my office, Miss McLean. Immediately."

"No I won't." She shoved him out of the way, unaware of the wide grins on the faces of the several people watching. She stepped into the elevator and punched the button for the lobby.

Red in the face, Mr. Simpson pointed a pudgy finger at her and blustered, "You're fired."

"Fine."

The doors slammed shut, cutting off any further comments Simpson might have made. As soon as he was out of sight, Lauren forgot him. He wasn't important, nor was her job. Amy was.

The phone in John's apartment rang a number of times that evening, then stopped. A few minutes later, it began ringing again, chiming repeatedly in the dark, empty rooms.

John looked at his watch. Nine-thirty. Where in hell was Lauren? he wondered, fear curling like a live thing in his stomach. A hundred suppositions ran wildly through his mind. She could have been in a car accident. Amy could be sick. Maybe Lauren had lost her keys to his apartment. Perhaps Lauren was ill.

He punched out Lauren's phone number. The irritating dull ring went on and on without anyone answering the phone. He hated the helpless feeling of not knowing what was happening back in Norfolk. The whole trip had been a complete waste of time. Not only had he been unable to see his ex-wife, but upon arriving in Los Angeles he had learned that one of the Status Brothers had been taken to the hospital for an emergency operation.

His next call was to the airport to try to get a flight out. A few minutes later he slammed the phone down and paced his hotel room. His luck was holding steady. There were no available flights until midmorning the next day.

He returned to the phone and punched out his home number with the same results as before.

John's flight had a short layover in Washington, D.C., before continuing on to Norfolk. He phoned Raytech from there and discovered to his amazement that Lauren didn't work for him any longer. His next call was to Amy's playschool. He was told Lauren had taken Amy out of the school the previous afternoon. His flight was called, and he was left with only questions and no answers.

When he finally arrived at Norfolk International Airport, he immediately went to the parking garage without bothering to make any more phone calls. The telephone had become an instrument of torture the last twenty-four hours. Either no one answered or they gave him information that only confused the situation. He needed action.

The two most important people in his life had disappeared. They had to be somewhere, and he would find them.

His plane had landed late in the afternoon, but he had enough time to go to Raytech before everyone left for the day. As soon as he smacked the door of his office open with his palm, he was swamped with a confusing assortment of people who had been waiting for him. His secretary he expected. Even Simpson's presence wasn't all that surprising. But the sight of his ex-wife perched on a chair in his office as though she had taken root put the cap on his day.

The following night Lauren sat on one of the redwood chairs on the porch of the cottage, staring out into the dark. Amy was asleep, but Lauren hadn't bothered going to bed herself, knowing it would be impossible for her to sleep. Doubt and indecision weighed heavily on her mind. Two days ago she had followed her instincts and gone to the playschool to prevent Amy's mother from taking her away.

Now she was having second thoughts about the wisdom of what she had done. Legally she had no right to decide what was best for Amy. She had virtually kidnapped the little girl, removing her not only from Norfolk but from the state of Virginia. Her reasoning at the time had been to hide Amy until John returned. If his ex-wife had taken Amy back to California, it might take him a long time to go through legal channels to get his daughter back.

She was so deep in thought she didn't hear the sound of car tires on the gravel driveway behind the cottage. Or the footsteps on the sandy ground. The first indication she had of a visitor was when she saw a shadowy figure come around the side of the cottage and stop at the bottom of the steps.

Dressed in jeans and a blue chambray shirt, John placed his hands on the porch rail and said casually, "You've had a busy couple of days."

Lauren launched herself out of her chair, throwing herself into his arms and nearly knocking him off balance. His arms came around her, holding her tightly, thankfully, against him, imprinting her slender frame on his.

It was enough just to hold her, to know she was all right. He felt moisture against his cheek and loosened his arms so he could see her face. Tears glistened on her lashes and her face as she raised her eyes to meet his. He kissed them away, finally taking her mouth with a desperate hunger.

When she buried her face in his neck, he lifted her and carried her back to the chair, settling her on his lap when he sat down. His hand went to her bare thigh, then stroked toward her hip.

"Good Lord, Lauren. You're practically naked."

"I wasn't expecting any company."

Only his shirt and her own thin nightshirt separated her breasts and his chest. Forcing his mind away from how good she felt, he asked, "How's Amy?"

"Confused."

He chuckled softly. "That's understandable. She's never been kidnapped before."

Lauren leaned back in his arms and gazed curiously at him. "You're taking all this very well. Why?"

With casual intimacy, he placed his hand on her bare upper thigh and left it there. "Did you expect me to be angry?"

"It was a possibility," she said, her voice wavering slightly.

"I admit I was a mite miffed when I kept calling my apartment and you didn't answer. Then I got worried. Why didn't you call me and let me know what was going on?"

"I didn't know where you were staying."

"My secretary did."

She dropped her gaze to the button of his shirt her fingers were toying with. Rather meekly she admitted, "I didn't even think of asking her."

"It's partly my fault. I was in such a hurry to get everything settled with Martine, I didn't think of leaving you a number where I could be reached either in San Francisco or in Los Angeles."

"Do you know why I brought Amy here? Your ex-wife was going to take Amy back to San Francisco." She paused. "One thing I haven't been able to figure out is how she knew where Amy was."

He sighed. "Mrs. Murray told her. Martine called the office, and Mrs. Murray had no reason not to tell her."

"Oh, well, I couldn't let her take Amy while you were gone. You left her in my care. I just couldn't let your ex-wife take her."

"Martine got what she wanted."

Lauren heard the taut anger in his voice. "Now I'm confused. I thought she wanted Amy. She doesn't have Amy."

"Amy was leverage to get what she really came after. The reason I couldn't come down here sooner was because I had to wait for the bank to open. I met Martine at my lawyer's office this morning to sign the papers to make Amy legally mine. My lawyer wasn't too happy with me since I got him out of bed in the middle of the night last night to get cracking on the paper work. After the papers were signed, I drove Martine to the airport. Then I was free to drive down here to get my missing women."

Lauren started to say something, then stopped.

Prodding her to finish what she was going to say, he said, "What?"

"I was going to ask if you had to pay your ex-wife before she would sign the custody papers, but I decided it wasn't really any of my business."

"You have a strange idea of what's your business and what isn't," he said with amusement. "You abscond with my daughter, losing your job in the process, and yet you shy away from asking about the arrangements I've made with my ex-wife."

"All right. Consider the question asked."

He nuzzled her neck, enjoying the subtle fragrance of her skin. "It was worth every penny."

"Did I make matters worse by taking Amy away?"

"Martine didn't appreciate it, but I did." His hand left her thigh and came up to cup her face. "How else would I have learned you were my fiancée?"

She lowered her gaze to his chest. "Oh, that."

"Yes, that." He stroked her throat, his fingers leaving a trail of heat. "Imagine my surprise when Martine told me my fiancée had taken Amy out of the playschool before she could get back there with the law."

His touch was taking her mind off what he was saying. Instead, she was concentrating on what she was feeling. "I suppose the woman at the playschool told your ex-wife who I said I was."

"I'm not complaining, Lauren." He brushed his mouth over hers, nipping her bottom lip with his teeth. "I am curious though. When were you going to tell me you were going to marry me?"

After all her previous protests about marriage, Lauren felt foolish. It would be even more ridiculous to attempt to deny her feelings at this point.

"I would have gotten around to it eventually. I'm still apprehensive about marriage, but I'm more scared of having to live without you. Maybe everybody feels like that. It's a gamble, but it's one I have to take." She wrapped her arms around his neck and pulled his head down. "Kiss me. I've missed you."

Accepting her invitation, he parted her lips with his tongue and took her mouth hungrily and hard.

Breaking away, he suddenly stood up, lifting her in his arms.

She gasped in surprise. "What are you doing?"

"I'm taking my fiancée to bed."

Lowering her voice as he carried her up the stairs to her bedroom, she said, "What if Amy wakes up and comes looking for me? She'll find us together in bed."

"She might as well get used to it, darling, since that's where she'll find us every night for the rest of our lives."

THE EDITOR'S CORNER

****

Get Ready For
A SPECTACULAR LOVESWEPT SUMMER

****

Next month we kick off one of LOVESWEPT's most sizzling summers! First, we bring you just what you've been asking for—

•

LOVESWEPT GOLDEN CLASSICS

•

We are ushering in this exciting program with four of the titles you've most requested by four of your most beloved authors . . .

•

Iris Johansen's
THE TRUSTWORTHY REDHEAD
(Originally published as LOVESWEPT #35)

•

Billie Green's
TEMPORARY ANGEL
(Originally published as LOVESWEPT #38)

•

Fayrene Preston's
THAT OLD FEELING
(Originally published as LOVESWEPT #45)

•

Kay Hooper's
SOMETHING DIFFERENT
(Originally published as LOVESWEPT #46)

•

With stunning covers—richly colored, beautifully enhanced by the golden signatures of the authors—LOVESWEPT'S GOLDEN CLASSICS are pure pleasure for those of you who missed them five years ago and exquisite "keepers" for the libraries of those who read and loved them when they were first published. Make sure your bookseller holds a set just for you or order the CLASSICS through our LOVESWEPT mail order subscription service.

And now a peek at our six new sensational romances for next month.

We start off with the phenomenal Sandra Brown's **TEMPERATURES RISING,** LOVESWEPT #336. Handsome Scout Ritland is celebrating the opening of a hotel he helped build on a lush South Pacific island when he's lured into a garden by an extraordinarily beautiful woman. But Chantal duPont has more in

(continued)

mind than a romantic interlude on this sultry moonlit night. She wants Scout all right—but to build a bridge, a bridge to connect the island on which she grew up with the mainland. Then there's an accident that Chantal never intended and that keeps Scout her bedridden patient. In the shadow of an active volcano the two discover their fierce hunger for each other . . . and the smoldering passion between them soon explodes with far-reaching consequences. This is Sandra Brown at her best in a love story to cherish. And remember—this wonderful romance is also available in a Doubleday hardcover edition.

Since bursting onto the romance scene with her enormously popular **ALL'S FAIR** (remember the Kissing Bandit?), Linda Cajio has delighted readers with her clever and sensual stories. Here comes an especially enchanting one, **DESPERATE MEASURES,** LOVESWEPT #337. Ellen Kitteridge is an elegant beauty who draws Joe Carlini to her as iron draws a magnet. Wild, virile, Joe pursues her relentlessly. Ellen is terrified because of her early loveless marriage to a treacherous fortune hunter. She runs from Joe, hides from him . . . but she can't escape. And Joe is determined to convince her that her shattered past has nothing to do with their thrilling future together. Linda's **DESPERATE MEASURES** will leave you breathless!

That brilliant new star of romance writing Deborah Smith gives you another thrilling story in *The Cherokee Trilogy,* **TEMPTING THE WOLF,** LOVESWEPT #338. This is the unforgettable tale of a brilliant, maverick Cherokee who was a pro football player and is now a businessman. Of most concern to Erica Gallatin, however, is his total (and threatening) masculinity. James is dangerous, perfection molded in bronze, absolutely irresistible—and he doesn't trust beautiful "non-Indian" women one bit! Erica is determined to get in touch with her heritage as she explores the mystery of Dove's legacy . . . and she's even more determined to subdue her mad attraction to the fierce warrior who is stealing her soul. This is a romance as heart-warming as it is heart-stopping in its intensity.

Judy Gill produces some of the most sensitive love stories we publish. In LOVESWEPT #339, **A SCENT OF ROSES,** she will once again capture your emotions with the exquisite romance of a memorable hero and heroine. Greg Miller is a race car driver who's lost his memory in an accident. His wife, Susan, puts past hurts aside when she agrees to help him recover. At his family's home in the San Juan Islands—a setting made for love—they rediscover the passion they shared . . . but can they

(continued)

compromise on the future? A thrilling story of deep passion and deep commitment nearly destroyed by misunderstanding.

It's always our greatest pleasure to discover and present a brand-new talent. Please give a warm, warm welcome to Courtney Henke, debuting next month with **CHAMELEON,** LOVESWEPT #340. This is a humorous yet emotionally touching romance we suspect you will never forget . . . in large measure because of its remarkable hero. Emma Machlen is a woman with a single purpose when she invades Maxwell Morgan's domain. She's going to convince the cosmetics mogul to buy the unique fragrance her family has developed. She's utterly desperate to make the sale. But she never counts on the surprises Max will have for her, not the least of which is his incredible attractiveness. Enchanted by Emma, drawn to her against his will, Max is turned upside down by this little lady whom he *must* resist. Emma has her work cut out for her in winning over Max . . . but the poor man never has a chance! An absolutely wonderful story!

And what could make for more sizzling reading than another of Helen Mittermeyer's Men of Fire? Nothing I can think of. All the passion, intensity, emotional complexity, richness, and humor you expect in one of Helen's love stories is here in **WHITE HEAT,** LOVESWEPT #341. When Pacer Dillon—that irresistible heartbreaker Helen introduced you to before—meets Colm Fitzroy, he is dead set on taking over her family business. She's dead set on stopping him. Irresistible force meets immovable object. Colm is threatened now, having been betrayed in the past, and Pacer is just the man to save her while using the sweet, hot fire of his undying love to persuade her to surrender her heart to him. Pure dynamite!

Enjoy all our LOVESWEPTs—new and old—next month! And please remember that we love to hear from you.

Sincerely,

Carolyn Nichols

Carolyn Nichols
Editor
LOVESWEPT
Bantam Books
666 Fifth Avenue
New York, NY 10103

BANTAM NEVER SOUNDED SO GOOD
NEW SUBLIMINAL SELF-HELP TAPES
FROM BANTAM AUDIO PUBLISHING

Invest in the powers of your mind.

Years of extensive research and personal experience have proved that it is possible to release powers hidden in the subconscious through the rise of subliminal suggestion. Now the Bantam Audio Self-Help series, produced by Audio Activation, combines sophisticated psychological techniques of behavior modification with subliminal stimulation that will help you get what you want out of life.

- ☐ 45106 **GET A GOOD NIGHT'S SLEEP . . . EVERY NIGHT: FEMALE** $7.95
- ☐ 45107 **GET A GOOD NIGHT'S SLEEP . . . EVERY NIGHT: MALE** $7.95
- ☐ 45041 **STRESS-FREE FOREVER: FEMALE** $8.95
- ☐ 45042 **STRESS-FREE FOREVER: MALE** $8.95
- ☐ 45081 **YOU'RE IRRESISTIBLE!: FEMALE** $7.95
- ☐ 45082 **YOU'RE IRRESISTIBLE!: MALE** $7.95
- ☐ 45004 **SLIM FOREVER: FOR WOMEN** $8.95
- ☐ 45005 **SLIM FOREVER: FOR MEN** $8.95
- ☐ 45022 **POSITIVELY CHANGE YOUR LIFE: FOR WOMEN** $7.95
- ☐ 45023 **POSITIVELY CHANGE YOUR LIFE: FOR MEN** $7.95
- ☐ 45035 **STOP SMOKING FOREVER: FOR WOMEN** $7.95
- ☐ 45036 **STOP SMOKING FOREVER: FOR MEN** $7.95
- ☐ 45094 **IMPROVE YOUR CONCENTRATION: WOMEN** $7.95
- ☐ 45095 **IMPROVE YOUR CONCENTRATION: MEN** $7.95
- ☐ 45112 **AWAKEN YOUR SENSUALITY: FEMALE** $7.95
- ☐ 45113 **AWKAEN YOUR SENSUALITY: MALE** $7.95
- ☐ 45130 **DEVELOP INTUITION: WOMEN** $7.95
- ☐ 45131 **DEVELOP INTUITION: MEN** $7.95
- ☐ 45016 **PLAY TO WIN: WOMEN** $7.95
- ☐ 45017 **PLAY TO WIN: MEN** $7.95
- ☐ 45010 **WEALTH, COME TO YOU: FEMALE** $7.95
- ☐ 45011 **WEALTH, COME TO YOU: MALE** $7.95

Look for them at your local bookstore, or use this handy page to order.

- -

Bantam Books, Dept. BAP4, 414 East Golf Road, Des Plaines, IL 60016

Please send me ______ copies of the tapes I have checked. I am enclosing $________ (please add $2.00 to cover postage and handling). Send check or money order—no cash or C.O.D.s please.

Mr/Ms ____

Address____

City/State ______________________________ Zip __________

BAP4—6/89

Please allow four to six weeks for delivery. This offer expires 12/89. Prices and availability subject to change without notice.

Special Offer
Buy a Bantam Book
for only 50¢.

Now you can have Bantam's catalog filled with hundreds of titles plus take advantage of our unique and exciting bonus book offer. A special offer which gives you the opportunity to purchase a Bantam book for only 50¢. Here's how!

By ordering any five books at the regular price per order, you can also choose any other single book listed (up to a $5.95 value) for just 50¢. Some restrictions do apply, but for further details why not send for Bantam's catalog of titles today!

Just send us your name and address and we will send you a catalog!

BANTAM BOOKS, INC.
P.O. Box 1006, South Holland, Ill. 60473

Mr./Mrs./Ms. ______________________
(please print)

Address ______________________

City ____________ State ____________ Zip ________

FC(A)—10/87

Please allow four to six weeks for delivery.